Dead Men Don't Get Married

by

Steve Shrott

For information, email **Cozy Cat Press**, cozycatpress@aol.com or visit our website at: www.cozycatpress.com

COZY CAT
PRESS

ISBN: 978-1-939816-50-4

Printed in the United States of America

Cover design by Nicole
http://www.covershotcreations.com

1 2 3 4 5 6 7 8 9 10

Many thanks to Patricia Rockwell for taking on this
project. I also want to express my gratitude to my
terrific parents and, in particular, my brother, Barry, for
his unwavering support.

Chapter One

I sauntered into my office, and saw Tanya, my receptionist, already working on the computer, a strange expression on her face. I tried to decode it, something that's almost as impossible as figuring out a Rubik's Cube or those instructions from Ikea. Then she started rapping her long, red fingernails on the desk, and I knew there'd be trouble.

"Listen, Arn," she said, fixing the collar on her bright yellow blouse. "About today..."

"You mean, *Easy Thursday*."

She moved close and whispered. "You know, sometimes, one Thursday may be a tad more difficult than another Thursday."

"What do you mean?"

She pointed toward my waiting room. My eyes popped open—it was packed like everyone was there to see Justin Beiber. "What's going on?"

She shrugged. "A lot of people needed you."

"Tanya, you have to say *no* sometimes."

"I do." She smiled proudly. "I cancelled two."

I rolled my eyes and sighed. I should have been used to it by now. Overbooking was her specialty.

"You got this." She handed me a small blue-tinted envelope.

"Thanks."

I was about to head to my office where I could look out the window, take in the breath-taking mountains of Corral, California, and forget that I had fifty people with bad teeth to see today.

"Open it."

I examined the envelope and glared at her. "It's already been opened."

"Just making sure there's no bombs inside."

"Bombs made by midgets?"

"Just read."

I removed a card and skimmed it. "It's from Debbie."

Tanya gave me an awkward smile. I looked at the card again and felt the color leave my face—forever.

She put her arm on my shoulder. "Look, Arnie, I know it's a shock. But you have to accept that your ex is getting married."

I tried to speak, but no words came.

"Okay, so you don't like the groom, and you're not that fond of orthodontists in general, and you don't want Debbie marrying anyone else ever, but you have to look on the bright side."

"What bright side?"

She didn't say anything for a moment, then shrugged.

There was no bright side. I should have been marrying Debbie. She was the one.

"Maybe you should take the morning off. I can reschedule the early patients."

I took a deep breath. I couldn't let my personal feelings interfere with my work. I was a dentist, for goodness' sake. I shook my head and stood up tall. "No, no. I'll see them. Who's up first?"

Tanya pretended to get busy, moving the one paper on her desk around like it was a nuisance.

"Tanya, who's in my office?"

She looked up, smiled. "Let's let that be a nice surprise."

Chapter Two

I expected the worst waiting for me and it turned out that way: Nathan Slatsky. Nine, cute, and really annoying. He had bright blue eyes that blinked a lot and brown hair that looked like he'd just come out of a wind tunnel. He wore a striped shirt with jeans, and yellow runners that didn't go with anything anyone ever wore in the history of the world.

"Hi, Nathan, how are you?" I said with as much enthusiasm as I could muster. Nathan, as usual, began asking a hundred questions. "How come you always wear that white coat, Dr. Katz?"

I put on a fake smile. "It's my favourite color."

"How come you have fillings and you're a dentist, Dr. Katz?"

"As a young boy, I didn't take care of my teeth."

"How come you became a dentist instead of an orthodontist Dr.—"

Orthodontist? He had to mention that word? My fake smile disappeared, and something inside snapped. "Do you know what happens to little boys who ask too many questions, Nathan?"

He shook his head.

I reached into the cupboard, pulled out a long needle and held it one inch away from my patient's now-petrified eyes.

At that moment, the door swung open, and Tanya marched in. Nathan suddenly shot back to life and whistled. "How come a be-au-ti-ful lady like you works with him?" He gave me a dismissive nod.

I glared at Tanya. "How come you get all the good questions?"

"What are you doing with that needle?"

"Just showing it to my patient. Thought he might like to see what I give people who can't sit quietly in their chairs." I moved the needle closer to Nathan, his face turning white.

Tanya grabbed my hand in a vice-like grip, and dragged me into the tiny back room where we keep all the dental supplies.

"What the hell are you doing, Arnie?"

"Just creating some rapport."

She exhaled sharply. "I know what's wrong."

"You mean with the youth of today?"

She leaned against some boxes of Dental Dam that had just been delivered and took a deep breath. That's the pose she had just before she gave Doctor Goldblatt, her previous employer, the black eye after he called her "sweetie" one too many times. I held up my arms for protection.

"It's about Debbie isn't it?"

I brought my arms down to my sides, but didn't relax them entirely. Just in case. I stared at her, realizing she might be onto something. "Maybe."

"You gotta get over this, Arnie. You can't be all freaked out when you go to the wedding. It's her special—"

"I'm not going to the wedding."

She raised her eyebrows. "Of course, you're going. I've already sent your RSVP. You're having the steak."

"I'm a vegetarian."

"Steaktofutti."

I hunched forward and shook my hands like a nervous drunk. "I can't go."

"She's your ex. You shared a lot of great memories together. The least you can do is be her friend."

"I don't want to be her friend."

"You are going, Arnie Katz."

"No. I'm not."

It was a match of wills but I knew the mentally stronger one of us would win.

Chapter Three

A day later, I sat third pew down in the Leamington United Church. Tanya sat beside me wearing a black lacy evening gown that looked much more expensive than something a receptionist, who makes what she does, should be wearing. I'd be hearing about that at the next salary negotiations. I gotta admit she did look lovely.

The small church had been around forever. It gave me a sense of awe just being inside. Of course, the seats were as hard as cement and I had a hunch that, after sitting here for an hour, my butt might need reupholstering.

As I looked at the platform where the wedding was going to take place, I realized the adult thing would be to realize it was over between Debbie and me. Of course, no one said I was an adult.

While Tanya and I waited for the service to begin, a croaky voice to my left whispered my name. I turned and stared into the moon-like face of an usher standing beside me. He seemed nice—if you like big, burly, bald men who speak out of one side of their mouths.

"Come with me."

"Where?" I asked, staring at his meat-hook hands that looked to be the size of roast chickens.

"Someone wants to see you."

"I don't go if I don't know where I'm going. You could be an alien taking me to the Planet Ripula to be probed."

Tanya pointed a red fingernail at me. "He's not from Ripula, although I'm not so sure you're not. Just go with the man."

I followed the big guy out into the hall and down a back corridor, past several doors. He stopped at the last one, knocked, then left me alone. I guess he didn't believe in the buddy system. A moment later, the door sprang open, and Debbie stood in front of me, a thousand-watt smile pulsating from her lips.

She looked amazing. She was squeezed into an arctic-white wedding dress, and gave off a look of ice-cold purity, and intoxicating beauty, all at once. I wanted to kiss her, and say, "let's get back together." But I knew it was too late for that.

She kissed me on the cheek. "Thanks for coming to the wedding, Arnie. I know that must have been difficult."

"No, no," I faked. "Wouldn't miss it for the world, been looking forward to it."

"Good. I, uh, wanted to talk to you about something."

I was puzzled. We hadn't spoken in a long time, and in a few moments, she'd be married. What was there to talk about?

I walked into the small room and sat down on one end of the couch, which was also as hard as granite. No one could sit there for long. The church had discovered a sneaky way to improve cardiovascular health.

Debbie took a seat on the other end of the couch, her body swivelled toward me. She pulled up her wedding dress so it wouldn't touch the ground.

"Arnie..."

"Uh huh."

She gulped. "I wanted to apologize for walking out on you. I really don't know what happened. I guess I just fell under Mickey's spell. I'm sorry."

That surprised me, but I guess before you get married there are things you needed to get off your chest. I blew out air. "You don't have to apologize; it's just something that happened. I wish you and Mickey the, uh, best."

"That's just it." She took out a tissue, wiped her eyes. "Do you think I'm making a mistake?"

"A mistake?"

"You know, by marrying him."

"I...do you love him?"

"I think so. But how do you really know?"

Doubt, she had doubt. The devil in my head said, "Tell her to call it off." The angel said, "Take a pill." Personally, I was leaning toward the devil's side. But I couldn't do it. "Look, I don't think I'm the right guy for this, Deb. Maybe you should talk to Tanya. She's really good with this stuff."

She slid closer to me on the sofa. "Arnie, you're one of the smartest people I know. Tell me if I'm doing the right thing."

I looked at her soft blue eyes for a moment, not sure what to say. "Tell her she's making the biggest mistake of her life!" screamed the devil. "Take a Xanax," said the angel. Great, I'm the only guy with a pill-pushing angel in his head.

I wanted her, but what could I do? I always believed that once a woman made her choice, there was no way back—especially on the eve of her wedding. "Yeah, you should marry Mickey."

"Thanks, Arnie." She wrapped her arms around me, and kissed my cheek.

I left Debbie, found my way out of the corridor without the help of burly guy, and moments later, sat back down beside Tanya. She, and the good-looking fellow sitting next to her were deep in conversation. I didn't know him, but it looked like he had some kind of hair weave. I wouldn't hold that against him because I'd never seen her so happy. Certainly not during work hours. Terrific, another couple to remind me of how perfect Debbie and I had been. I sat in silence as I listened to Tanya tell him how a receptionist was the most important person in the dentist's office—much more important than the dentist. How that worked, I wasn't quite sure.

Her conversation started to wind down and she leaned toward me, whispering, "What did Debbie want?"

"How'd you know it was her?"

"A woman knows."

"She just, uh, wanted to make sure I'm okay."

"And are you?"

I shrugged. "I have to be."

She nodded, knowing, I'm sure, that I wasn't okay.

"Oh, by the way, this is Rick," she said, pointing to Mr. Hair Weave. He reached his hand out, shook mine, and I noticed a Patek Philippe watch on his wrist.

"He's an old friend of Debbie's."

I planned to ask about the watch, but a moment later, instead of the wedding march, and Debbie sauntering down the aisle, two policemen appeared and whispered something to a tall man on the podium.

The man, blank-faced, smoothed the labels of his black jacket, and brought out a microphone.

"Excuse me, everyone. I have an important announcement—I'm afraid the wedding has been cancelled."

Murmurs and gasps.

"I've just been informed by the police that the groom, Mickey Harrison, is dead."

Chapter Four

I felt bad for Debbie, but I let her friends and family comfort her. I was no longer a part of her inner circle. I may have once been her lover, but now I was just a friend. Soon, I'd probably be an acquaintance, then "who are you?"

The police seemed to be in control of everything so I headed home.

I entered my building, The Harkin Towers, and trudged up to my apartment. I peeked inside the terrarium on my coffee table, and said hello to my turtle, Humphrey. Then I sat on the couch and stared at the lithographs on the wall. Some of my favorite painters—Dali, Van Gogh, Lautrec. Usually, they gave me lots of pleasure. Not today.

That night, I had trouble sleeping, but finally dozed off. I awoke to someone pounding on my door. I got up, still exhausted, wondering who the hell it could be so early in the morning.

I opened the door to find Gino Samatini.

How to describe him? The word "ginormous" comes to mind. He looked like he spent eighty hours a week in the gym, bench-pressing Toyotas, and the rest of the time eating fried chicken by the bucket. He had black stringy hair that fell onto his shoulders. He seldom blinked, making it look like he always had his eye on you. He probably did.

"Hey, Arnie."

"Gino?" I said, wiping the sleep from my eyes, not to mention a whole lot of sesame seeds from eating that

Sesame Delight Bar in bed the previous night. "Is it my imagination or is it six thirty in the morning?"

"No, not your imagination. Mr. Rodrico wants to see you."

"About what?"

"That would be better left for Mr. Rodrico to explain. Get your clothes on and let's go."

I nodded and got dressed. You didn't argue with Gino or Rodrico and live to tell about it. I slid into Gino's limo and, a few moments later, we were on the road.

As he drove, we exchanged small talk about his car, the weather, some of his business associates who seemed to have died in strange accidents lately, and, of course, his hobby of collecting doilies, some of which he crocheted himself. He apparently had about 300 in his collection—all colors, shapes and designs. The other mob members must be so jealous.

After a few minutes, he changed the subject.

"Listen, doc, I got a tooth in the back that's killing me. Can you take a look at it?"

"Sure, Gino. Call my office and we'll set something up."

"I meant now."

"Now, while the car is moving?"

"I'm trying to make good time. You know how Mr. Rodrico hates tardiness."

"How about we pull over for a minute? I'll take a quick peek."

"Yeah, I guess." He parked on the side of the road and I examined his chipped, yellowed teeth.

"I think I see the problem, Gino." I reached into my pocket and pulled out my dental tweezers. I slid them into his mouth and removed a large popcorn kernel that had been stuck between his teeth. "How's that feel?"

"Much better. Thanks a lot, doc. You're a genius."

"Listen, Gino, why don't you make an appointment sometime at my office? I spotted a few cavities."

His expression suddenly changed, and I swear I saw his bottom lip tremble. "Is it gonna hurt?"

I managed to calm him down and gave him my office number.

You may wonder why I would actually solicit business from a mobster. It's funny, but I can't stop myself. Whenever I see someone with dental problems, I just have to fix them. No matter who it is.

We arrived at Rodrico's house, just as I finally convinced Gino that his trip to my office wouldn't hurt and he might even get a free sucker out of it. That seemed to make him happy.

The house, an older brownstone in a suburban neighbourhood, looked quaint, but not the type of dwelling you'd think the head of a mob family would inhabit. And they had really kept it up. It had been repainted in the spring after a revenge bombing by Jimmy the Fruit, (he liked killing by putting explosives in bananas,) and the hole in the roof repaired last Christmas when Larry the Ferret, (he was a master at hiding in small spaces,) slid down the chimney dressed as Santa, only with an Uzi.

I walked inside. Lisa, the maid, said hello, and told me I should go down the hall into the study.

The study resembled a library with its tall bookcases and tables piled high with magazines. The big man sat at his mahogany desk reading a book on nuclear physics. Most people might be surprised that a man in Rodrico's position would be a reader. But he was very knowledgeable about many things other than whacking people.

His coal black hair and dimples made him look much younger than his sixty-odd years. Today, as usual, he dressed in a black suit and black tie.

He stood up from his desk, came over and shook my hand. "Great to see you, Arnie."

"Thanks, Mr. Rodrico." I suppose when he discussed mob business with his associates he had a dour expression, but with me, he usually smiled.

"How's the teeth business going?"

"Good, great."

"As I've told you before, we could put you under contract and make you mob dentist. Pay you really well. You could take care of all the guys. Of course, you'd have to give up your other clients."

"I appreciate it." And I did. But my mind already whirled with newspaper headlines—'Arnie Katz, mob dentist, murdered today over a root canal that went bad.' Somehow, I didn't see my future that way. "Still thinking about it, Mr. Rodrico."

"Have a seat," he said, pointing toward a red velvet chair in front of his desk. I sat as he walked behind the desk, and paced back and forth. And I have to tell you when a member of a major criminal organization paces, it puts you on edge.

"The assignment I have for you today is more of a personal matter, rather than business. I wouldn't trust this with too many people, Arnie, but—you—you're like family."

"Thank you," I said, not sure I wanted to be part of 'the family.'

He paced again. No wonder he was in such great shape, what with all the pacing.

Suddenly, he stopped and pursed his lips. "It's my wife, you know, Judy."

I nodded.

He sat down, picked up a file and rifled through the papers inside like it was a marked deck of cards and he wanted to find an ace. "See, lately I've received reports that she's been seen in the company of a young man. As yet, we haven't identified him. But if she's having an affair, I want to know." He banged his fist hard on the desk.

Rodrico loved Judy. But I wondered what would happen if he found out she'd been having an affair. I really didn't want to be responsible for any bad things that happened. So I did the manly thing and tried to weasel out of this assignment.

I stood up as if I were about to go. "You know, Mr. Rodrico, I'm not sure if I'd be very helpful. I'm not a specialist in this kind of work."

He stared at me, his eyes intense, then moved his face close to mine. I'm sure it was the same way he approached someone right before he gave them the kiss of death.

I moved out of smooch range.

"Arnie, I want you to do this for me as a favor."

"I would love to but the thing is..."

He stared some more. Sweat poured out of places on my body I didn't know you could sweat from. "Okay, fine. I'll do it.

Chapter Five

The next day, Debbie called. "Arnie, I have to talk to you about something."

"Are you sure now's the right time? I mean, it's only been a day since..."

"Please, meet me."

An hour later, we were at The Station House, a coffee place in the village that we used to frequent.

She showed up wearing a blue halter top and tartan skirt, a tissue in her hands. Every few moments, she wiped her eyes.

"The police say a generator exploded in Mickey's orthodontist office and that's what made the place catch fire." She started to weep again. "He doesn't have any other family, so they gave me his ashes." She reached into her purse and produced a mayonnaise jar.

I stared at it puzzled.

"Originally, he was in a cremation urn, but it seemed so impersonal. Mickey loved mayo and I thought he might feel more comfortable here."

I patted her shoulder, understanding.

"Arnie, this must have been another of those creepy murders going on in the city."

"You mean, 'The Orthodontist Killings'?"

"Yeah. He must be some crazy to strangle the victims with the same wire they use for braces."

"Arch wire."

"What?"

"The wire they use for braces."

She tilted her head to one side as if that would help her understand better. "Does it matter? Totally innocent orthodontists are being killed. Shouldn't someone be looking into this?"

"I don't think Mickey was killed by the same guy. First of all, the police didn't find any of the arch wire, and second...you said yourself a generator exploded."

"It was probably a subterfuge. He's trying to confuse everyone. You know he's killed a few orthodontists one way, now he's trying to switch it up."

"I'm not sure murderers 'switch it up.' They usually stick to the tried and true. Regardless, we should leave this to the police." I held up my hands, palms facing her in the universal sign for, "I'm not getting involved."

"But you're a detective."

"Part-time detective. The police are full time. They can handle it."

"You mean like they handled that lunatic who stole creampuffs from all the bakeries in Corral. It went on for weeks with no results. And then the chief's son confesses. You'd think someone would have noticed he went from a hundred and twenty pounds to two hundred and forty in a week."

"Actually, they arrested him thinking he'd been using cocaine because they found white powder on his upper lip. Turns out it was the icing sugar from a creampuff."

I could see Debbie's thoughts had drifted elsewhere. "Look, Arnie, Mickey wouldn't want me to go to the police."

"Why not?"

"He didn't like them. Said they were involved in all kinds of conspiracies."

It sounded like Mickey all right. "Debbie, I'm not comfortable handling this case. It involves an ortho...I don't think I'd do a good job."

Debbie slipped her hand in mine. "Can you do it—for me?"

I looked at her sad eyes. How could I refuse? "Okay, sure, I'll spend a little time on it. But don't expect much."

She reached into her purse and handed me a key ring.

"These are for his apartment. Maybe there's some clues there."

"Great." I reached over to take the keys, but it seemed like they were crazy-glued to her hand.

She shrugged. "We could start there anyways."

I removed my fingers from the keys, getting a bad feeling. "We?"

"Wanna take my car or yours?"

"My car, because I'm the only one who's going."

"I need to go with."

"Debbie, it might be dangerous."

I could see I'd made an impression on her. She swooped up the mayo jar from the table, dropped it into her purse, stood, and said, "Let's go."

I rolled my eyes, made exasperating noises. But I knew from experience not to argue with her. Once she'd made up her mind, my only recourse was to fly the white flag.

Chapter Six

Mickey lived in a large white-bricked house near The Trundle Path, one of the wealthier areas in Corral. His almost mansion-like house stood next to an extra wide drive-way. On either side, a marble lion's head glared at you, as if it were feeding time and you were lunch.

Debbie opened the front door and elegance greeted us. Crystal glass-ware decorated the long rectangular dining room table and art nouveau paintings hung on the walls with special blue lights above them.

On the floor lay a Persian rug with colors so vibrant it resembled a painting itself. It must have cost a small fortune. Of course, I always wonder why people spend so much money on something that everyone's going to walk all over. As I took in all the incredible wealth that surrounded us, I thought that maybe I should have become an orthodontist. Of course, then I realized I had become insane for a moment, and got the voices in my head to talk me down.

I yelled, "Hello?" No answer.

"What are you doing?" Debbie asked.

"Just want to make sure we're alone."

She pulled the mayo jar out of her purse and pointed to it. "Mickey's here, remember?"

"Right."

We decided to walk upstairs and see if we could learn anything more. When we reached the top, we realized that while downstairs seemed pristine and untouched, upstairs had something else going on. There were four bedrooms and each had furniture overturned, papers scattered on the floor and broken mirrors. Lots of them. Someone had some serious bad luck ahead of them—especially the guy who had to clean this up. I surmised that a couple of goons had been here searching for something, but I decided to soft-peddle it for Debbie. "Mickey didn't have the greatest housekeeper, eh?"

She didn't say anything.

"Which one is Mickey's bedroom?"

She pointed to a closed door that I hadn't seen. I tried to open it, but it wouldn't budge.

"Mickey always kept it locked. Said he had some valuable things in there."

Something didn't add up. The goons had destroyed the rest of the second floor, but they didn't touch a room where the valuable stuff was located? They should be ashamed to call themselves goons. "Do you have the key for this room?"

She examined her key ring. "No, I know all these and what they're for. That one's not here."

I wanted to find out what was in the room, but I didn't want Debbie with me in case it turned out to be disturbing. So I left it for now. The two of us walked down the hall to Mickey's office. The messer-uppers had been here too. Desk drawers had been removed and over-turned, paintings destroyed and pieces of them dumped everywhere. One photo that still hung on the wall was of a woman in a revealing bathing suit. I recognized her—Stephanie Warwick. Several years ago, she had acted in B-movies with titles like 'Stella Lopez and The Case of the Haunted Bikini.' I had been a big fan along with every other horny sixteen-year-old male on the planet. The movies dried up after a while and I had always wondered what had happened to her.

On top of Mickey's large oak desk, lay books dealing with psychology, medicine and politics. I had no idea Mickey had so much depth. What sounded more likely is that if I checked the insides of the hard covers, I'd find comic books. When we were rooming together, that's all he read—except, of course, for *Playboy*. He claimed it was important for an orthodontist to know anatomy.

I knelt down to look at one of the drawers and found his appointment book. On today's page, I read, 'call Stephanie W. at two. Bring roses.'

I froze for a moment, stunned. Could Mickey be seeing the same Stephanie as in the photo? I found that hard to believe. Never figured a woman like her would go for him. Sure, he was a professional, but he was kind of an idiot-savant. More idiot than savant. I knew I couldn't tell Debbie about Mickey's possible "other" girl, but I had to talk to Stephanie. I wrote her phone number down in my notebook.

A moment later, I sensed Debbie hovering over my shoulder.

"What are you writing down?"

"Uh, just a phone number."

"Whose?"

"Someone Mickey had an appointment to meet."

"What's his name? I knew most of his friends."

"Uh, Steph..." I stopped suddenly.

"Steph?"

I nodded.

"What kind of name is that?"

"Swedish, I think."

"Oh. Well. I don't know him."

"I think we should go," I said, wanting to get Debbie out of there. "I don't think we'll find anything that will help us anyway." We walked out of the room, down the stairs and out the front door.

Debbie brought out her key to lock the door.

"Oh, listen, I have to go to the washroom; I'll be back in a sec."

"Sure, I'll wait in the car."

I dashed up the stairs and removed a carver from my pocket. It's great at removing plaque from under the gum line, but it's also useful in removing a goon from his gun. I shoved the sharp end into the lock of the locked room and turned it to the right, then several times to the left. The door clicked open.

I threw the carver into my pocket, and opened the door.

I looked around, checked the closet, every drawer in the desk, under the bed—everywhere in the room. I found nothing valuable.

It didn't make sense.

Chapter Seven

I left Mickey's house, dropped Debbie off at her place and went home. She spent most of the trip figuring out what we should do next. I spent most of the trip figuring out how I got into this mess.

The next day, I had Tanya move my patients to the afternoon so that I could get to work on Rodrico's case. It's probably not a good idea to keep a mob boss waiting. She wasn't happy about it and started to lecture me, when I told her I had to go, as my other phone was ringing. That's when I learned something about myself—it hurts when I make fake ringing sounds with my lips.

Rodrico had informed me that Judy always left early on Tuesday mornings, claiming she went shopping with her girlfriends. So I drove over to their house, parked across the road and waited.

I didn't often do stake-outs. They usually wasted a lot of time and you never knew if they would lead anywhere or not. However, today the time went fast. Fifteen minutes later, Judy, exited wearing a sexy short blue skirt and red heels. She wore her coal black hair tied in the back, which seemed to highlight her high cheekbones. Her face had this determined kind of look—like Indiana Jones when he searched for the Temple of Doom or every woman when she's trying to find the right pumps. She slid into her midnight black Lexus.

I followed her to the Southgate Mall, a new shopping center that had opened up in Corral a few weeks ago. Three floors, it had everything from the latest in electronic toys for executives to fashions for pets. She sauntered inside and I trailed her as she ping-ponged in and out of various clothing and accessory shops. So far, nothing out of the ordinary.

She bought several pieces of pink lingerie at Fancy Dan's, a hip new fashion emporium. Since I had time, I checked out a few of the new items for a fashionista like myself. Although I'm not sure if the world will ever be ready for a dentist in a kilt.

About eleven, she left the mall and took the Leslie Freeway to Dunning, then turned off onto Daglan Ave. She parked and walked into The Palace Restaurant, a new place catering to the beautiful and rich.

I walked in and looked for Judy but the room seemed to swallow her up whole. A moment later, a French *maître d'* appeared. He looked at me like a customer at the dollar store deciding if a pen was worth the buck. A moment later, he'd apparently made that decision, and it was a no.

"Excuse me, sir, do you have a reservation?"

"Uh, no, I don't," I said, looking past him, continuing to search for Judy.

"I'm sorry. We're full."

And yet I saw several empty tables. I guess that's where the invisible people sat. They don't tip as much, but you didn't get too many complaints from them either.

I tried to stall to give me more time to find Judy, but French-ie seemed determined to get me out of his establishment. He crossed his arms, and gave me a smug look that said, don't come back unless you have a million dollars and a face lift.

Just as I was about to leave, I caught a flash of Judy sitting with several girls. They were about same age as Judy and equally fashion conscious. All had drinks in front of them. Maybe, hubby had been wrong about her; maybe she was just out with her friends.

I left and phoned Rodrico on my cell. "Everything seems fine, Mr. Rodrico. Judy's only been with her girlfriends."

"I want you to stay on the case until you find out who the guy is."

"It doesn't look like there is any guy."

He paused a moment, then his voice sounded hard. "You'll find him, Arn, or..." He hung up. He didn't complete that last sentence. He didn't have to. That "or" implied so many things. None of them good.

Chapter Eight

The next morning, I went into the office and had a full day. I fit dental implants, filled a few cavities and taught some patients the intricacies of tongue cleaning. Believe me, it's an art in the right hands. Although personally, I prefer the art that the elephants produce when they put paint on their trunks and splash it on canvas. Sometimes it's hard to tell what the picture is, but I have a feeling it has something to do with peanuts.

At lunch time, I called Stephanie Warwick's number but no one answered. I was about to head out for lunch when Tanya burst into my office and asked if I remembered about Friday.

I crinkled my brow. "Is it that there's only going to be one person instead of ten booked for the nine o'clock appointment?"

She said, "Nooooo," as if that was the most outrageous thing in the world to expect.

"Your speech."

"My speech?"

"You know, the Dental Association. They're honoring you."

"Oh, right, right."

"How's it coming?"

"Fine, great."

"Is it finished?"

"Not quite yet."

"Have you started it?"

I gave her my innocent look. "I'd rather not say for fear that someone might hurt me physically or mentally." She stared at me a moment, and I thought it could go either way—physically or mentally.

"Arnie, this has to be good. It's not every day you get voted dentist of the year."

She sat down looking like a queen awaiting someone being thrown to the lions. And when I say, someone, I mean me.

"I'd like to hear it."

"Well, you know, I said, 'almost.' It's not completely finished yet."

"Arnie, it's on Friday. Let me hear what you have. Maybe I can offer suggestions."

"Fine." I reached into the filing cabinet and removed the file with my speech. I leaned against the wall, about to start when Tanya motioned to me.

"Stand like you're at the event. I want to get the full picture."

I straightened my posture and cleared my throat. "Hello everyone." I looked at Tanya, suddenly feeling gobs of sweat dripping down my forehead. "Thank you for presenting me with this amazing award. Actually, I felt nervous coming here today—much like a patient before his first root canal."

I smiled at Tanya, waiting for the big laugh. She just stared. Maybe she didn't hear me. I repeated, "Like a patient before his first root canal."

Still, no laugh. As a matter of fact, Tanya looked at me like she was at the funeral of someone rich who didn't leave her any money.

"Go on."

"That's it, so far."

Her eyes seemed to get this intensity around them. It reminded me of a bull when he saw something red. I just hoped she wouldn't charge at me.

"It's in four days, Arnie. You gotta move on this."

"It's just...I've been busy with a few things."

Her eyes softened and she moved toward me. I moved back, just in case it was a trick. I didn't think she'd hurt me intentionally, but sometimes her arms did things her brain didn't know about.

"Arnie, I understand."

"You do?"

"I know you always hoped Debbie would come back to you. But that's probably not going to happen. She made her choice, and although Mickey is gone, you've got to respect that decision. For some reason she thought he was the right guy for her. The best thing for you to do now is start dating other people. I know this nice girl over at my lawyer's office and she—"

"You have a lawyer?"

"Yeah, for contract negotiations. You know, in case certain employers don't toe the line." She glared at me, indicating that perhaps, maybe, in some very obscure way, she was talking about me.

"Thanks for the concern, Tanya. But I'm really not into dating right now."

"Okay, but give it some thought, alright. Maybe you'll feel differently, you know, in the future."

"Sure."

She smiled and marched out the door. Although it looked like Tanya had just let that dating thing go, I had a hunch she'd subtly bring it up again, not so much in words as one night maybe kidnapping me, then airlifting my body to a speed-dating event in downtown Corral.

On my break I made a call.

"Hello, Stephanie, I'm a friend of Mickey Harrison. I wonder if I could talk to you about him."

Her voice sounded just as I remembered it from the movies—lyrical, sensual...a melody.

"Do you know where he is?"

"Uh, no, not exactly. That's why I wanted to speak to you." Of course, I had told her a bit of a fib. I knew exactly where Mickey was—in the murky depths of a mayonnaise jar. But sometimes to get at the truth, you can't be completely honest.

"I'm at 37 Whitmeyer Lane."

"Okay, how about seven?"

"That sounds fine."

A few hours later, I sat on a buttery-soft sofa in Stephanie's apartment. You know, one of those sofas where you sink right in, and feel about five inches shorter than when you walked into the room.

The living room radiated a sense of warmth, but no movie-star vibe. Nothing ostentatious, no Oscars. Although, I'm not sure, 'Stella Lopez and The Case of the Haunted Bikini.' was in the running.

She did have a wall-shelf that housed several interesting objects that looked like they were from another time—a small clay rock that had been chiselled into the shape of a horn, a bracelet with tiny paintings of animals, and a square ring with an engraved purple stone.

Stephanie still had the golden hair, glimmering eyes, and perfect complexion. She reminded me of the beautiful princesses you read about in fairy tales that you never thought you'd actually meet in real life.

I was only concerned about one thing. In her last movie, she played a wacko beauty queen who murdered a detective. I hoped that was just acting.

I told her how much I loved her movies.

"Thanks. But I'm out of the industry now."

"Oh, what are you doing?"

"Different things. Taking classes...sales." Other than movies, sales might be the perfect job for her. I bet with her looks she could sell the bible to atheists.

She smiled, showing the perfect ratio of teeth to lip. "How did you meet Mickey?"

"Well, I needed some dental work done, and I found Mickey's ad in the yellow pages."

She leaned back in her Morris chair and seemed to relax. That always got me worried. When people relaxed it could mean one of two things: 1) They were relaxed. I figured that one out by myself. Or 2) They were pretending to be relaxed so that you wouldn't know they weren't relaxed. That meant they were hiding something. Being a PI was a tough business.

"After a few visits to Mickey, I don't know, I guess I just fell in love with him. He had that charm, that magnetism, that—"

"Yeah, yeah," I said, getting slightly irritated. "He was great, I know."

Then she said something that hit me like the Sriracha Sauce at The Tamale Hut.

"We were supposed to be married a week ago."

Chapter Nine

I couldn't believe it. Mickey had planned to marry Stephanie too? That was one marriage too many. I didn't think even he would stoop to that. Debbie would be heartbroken if she knew.

"When did you see him last?" I asked.

"A few days ago. We had plans to meet yesterday but he didn't show. Of course, that wasn't unusual. Sometimes he gets carried away with some great new dental innovation he's working on. Did you know he invented an electric toothbrush that can be used in the bedroom for other purposes? He was in the last stages, trying to figure out how to cut down on the overheating, and the sparks."

"I could see where that might be a problem."

"When someone's a genius like him, you don't want to disturb—"

I inhaled loudly around the part where she called Mickey a genius, hoping the sound would drown it out. It didn't.

She stood up, began walking around the room. "But he didn't phone this time and that was different. I called him at the office and at home, but no answer. Then I went to his place." She stopped moving and stared at me. "He wasn't there. I panicked, hired a PI. Mickey never liked..."

"Yeah, I know; the police are into conspiracies."

"Right. Anyway, the PI couldn't find any trace of Mickey. Finally, I had to accept that something had happened to him." She wiped her eyes.

I spent the next several minutes struggling up out of the sofa to get my height back again. When I stood, I felt like I was still missing a few inches.

I thanked Stephanie for talking to me and asked her for the name of the PI she'd hired. I'd never heard of him—Richard Levinsky. She said to get in touch if I found out anything.

I got in my car and left a message at the PI firm of Levinsky and Schwartz. I hung up, and two seconds later, the phone rang.

"Hello," I said, wondering what took Levinsky or Schwartz, so long to get back to me. Only it wasn't either of them.

"Hello, Mr. Rodrico."

"Arnie, I just got a tip that Judy's meeting someone at the The Red Pickle Restaurant on Valley Road."

Chapter Ten

The Red Pickle was a chain that had been around forever. The waitresses all wore hats and shoes in the shape of pickles. They got newspaper coverage when one of the waitresses got drunk outside and the headline read—'Red Pickle Waitress Pickled.'

Each booth had a fixture with bright lights flooding the table. It was almost like they wanted you to confess to some crime—"It was me. I ordered the fish sticks!"

There were pictures of pickles all over the walls, on the tables, in the menu. After you'd left here, you pretty well didn't want to see another pickle the rest of your life. I easily got a seat in the back, away from Judy and her posse of girlfriends. Next to me, some children were celebrating a birthday party. Things seemed to be going swimmingly until the clown's big red nose fell into the cake, and no one wanted seconds after that.

About fifteen minutes later, Judy's girlfriends split and a tall, thin man appeared.

He looked about forty, dark-skinned with a small scar on the side of his cheek. His black hair was combed back like the old movie stars used to do. He had a slightly lop-sided smile that only added to his charm. Judy wrapped her arms around him, then they sat down at a table together.

I had trained in body language and could usually tell the difference between a regular guy and a crook just by the way they moved. Regular guys moved easily, naturally. Crooks generally seemed more stiff, cautious, worried that the extra large meatball on their plate might be a bomb and could go *kaboom* at any moment. That could give anyone indigestion.

I got the crook vibe from Judy's guy.

The average person would probably say he and Judy were simply a couple having a nice meal at a restaurant. He had his arm around her and she often looked into his eyes and smiled. But something seemed wrong. And the thought that kept coming back to me was that they weren't having an affair, but that they might be plotting something. Rodrico wouldn't be happy to hear that.

Lop-sided had almost finished his drink and they started having an animated conversation. Him, moving his upper body back and forth. Her, bending toward him, spreading her hands. I expected a tango to break out at any moment. But all that happened was that they stood and kissed one another. The kiss seemed a little odd too. It wasn't the kiss of a couple having an affair. It was more of a...I don't know what.

Judy stayed at the restaurant, but lop-sided left. I followed. I needed a picture to show Rodrico. He went to the parking lot slid into what looked to be a new white BMW. I got into my Acura, upset that all the bad guys had such cool cars.

He turned onto Stevens Road, then headed down to Stinson. He crossed the Hamley Bridge, and took the Venata interchange to Rexton Street. Twenty minutes later, after forcing me to zigzag all over town, he stopped at a large house on Dunkirk. We were in the Ridley Path area where a lot of soccer moms lived. I parked across the street, trying to fit in, although I'd probably need a minivan and cleavage to really make it work.

When lop-sided left his car, I took out my camera phone and snapped a few shots. He looked back and I quickly slid down the seat so he wouldn't see me.

When I popped up again, the scene had changed—a fifty-ish, angular man wearing a porkpie hat walked out to greet my subject. He was Phil Chimera, the boss of The Daroga Mob Family.

This was not good news for Rodrico, who headed up the Larota Family on the other side of town.

Chapter Eleven

I didn't want to have a gang war on my conscience so I decided to hold off telling Rodrico this latest update. At least until I knew a little more.

I went home and decided to relax. I lay back on my couch watching "Castle" reruns when the phone rang.

"Can I come over?"

"Something wrong, Debbie?"

"No, I just wanna talk."

"Uh, sure."

Twenty minutes later, she stood beside me wearing a yellow silk blouse and, what looked to be green leggings. A little strange, but when I mismatch clothes, I call it a fashion statement. The statement I'm trying to make is, "help, I can't dress myself." Debbie is usually well put together, so this whole Mickey thing must really be freaking her out.

She kept wiping her already red eyes which made them even redder. She hugged me tight, then planted a soft, sweet kiss on my lips. It felt wonderful. The memories of us together came flooding back into my now oxytocin-filled brain. I wanted to kiss her back, but I knew it wasn't right.

"What's wrong, Arnie?"

"I don't think you're over Mickey yet."

"I am, I am," she said, puckering up again.

"Sit down, Debbie."

She looked at me, puzzled, then plopped onto the couch, the pucker gradually fading away.

"Mickey's death just happened a few days ago. I don't think your brain has sorted it all out yet."

She thought a moment, then shrugged. "Maybe you're right. I do kind of feel like I'm about to explode."

"That's understandable. You were on your way to be married to the man you loved when all this weird stuff went down."

"I'm not sure that's it at all." She looked at her leggings for a moment. Perhaps, re-evaluating the look.

"Maybe I feel bad because I chose the wrong man in the first place." She grabbed my hand.

I sat down beside her on the couch, not knowing how to respond to that.

"Did you love me, Arnie?"

I didn't have to think twice. "Of course, I did."

"So why aren't we together now?"

"Things happened."

"That's really deep."

"Look, you probably felt that Mickey was the better choice for you."

"Then why don't I feel something in here?" She touched her chest. "Okay, sure, I'm upset he's gone. But I don't feel bad we're not together."

"You need to sort all this out, Debbie. We'll talk about it another time."

She nodded, muttered, "sure, sure," then turned around, and walked out the door, without saying another word. I know she'd give some deep thought to what I said—and then ignore it completely.

I went into my small home office and sat at the desk. I looked at some of the rare detective novels on my bookcase, and realized that despite all the stress and tension I had experienced, I was happy I had become a PI.

I reached into my jacket pocket and felt for my notebook. I'd made notes on my cases and thought I would go over them. But the notebook wasn't there. I checked a few other pockets. Not there either. I figured I had left it at the office.

I was about to head out to get it, but then noticed a postcard on the carpet by the door. I hadn't seen it when I'd entered so it must have just arrived. I picked it up, and saw that on one side, was a picture of Grauman's Chinese Theatre, and on the other, words cut from the pages of a magazine. They said, "Meet me at The Three Rings Restaurant on Wickens Rd, tomorrow at twelve midnight, if you want to stay healthy." It was signed, "Z."

Chapter Twelve

Like the note said, that night I headed over to The Three Rings Restaurant. It was located near Vacara Avenue, that wonderful part of town where people would shoot you for a quarter. Don't ask what they'd do for a dollar.

Parts of the neon sign out front had burned out years ago and the name now read, "Th Thr Rin Restaurant."

I entered the large room that resembled a gymnasium more than a restaurant, and the first thing I noticed were the pictures on the walls depicting their numerous specials. Their 'Meatloaf Supreme' looked delicious in the photos, except for the green parts. I hoped it was an old photo rather than old meat.

Long tables covered with white paper tablecloths filled the room. The clientele were a mix of the young and old—some were passed out on the tables, their heads soaking up the atmosphere, and maybe some saliva that dribbled down the side of their mouths. Others looked like their future career path pointed to them being passed out on the tables. Dare to dream.

I edged toward a dark corner where a man sat. I figured he was 'Z,' mostly because, unlike the others, he seemed actually alive. He was dressed in a red sports jacket, no tie. Hard to believe management had a no tie policy here. On his head he wore a turban. Sunglasses and a black beard completed the look, that I'm sure was going to be copied by every metro-sexual in America. He swayed back and forth, looking like the python in a snake charmer's basket.

I walked over to his table. "You, Z?"

He nodded, then spoke in a strange accent I'd never heard before. It sounded like a combination of Moroccan, French and Italian. "Sit."

I sat down on the flimsy metal chair. A moment later, a zaftig waitress with the name *Sarah* on the card pinned to her chest, came by to take my order.

"Green tea," I said.

She looked at me like I'd requested plutonium. "We got Earl Grey, you want it?"

"Yeah, that's okay."

"What else?"

"That's it," I said.

She left annoyed. I could tell customer service was a priority here.

I looked at the man sitting in front of me. I'd guessed his age to be around thirty-five years old. Although outwardly calm, almost stoic, I sensed inner anxiety. "So what do you want?" I asked.

He licked his thick lips for a moment, then spoke slowly, again, in that weird accent. "You must stop looking into the death of this man you call Mickey."

"Why?"

"Very bad things could happen to you if you continue."

I stared at him, trying to stifle the surprise in my voice. "Sorry, I can't do that. I promised someone close to me that I would find out what happened to him."

The man remained motionless for a moment, then removed his wallet. "I will give you money."

"I don't want money."

He gave me a stern look or maybe a killer's look. I didn't know which, and it's probably a mistake to get those two confused. A chill walked up my spine, vertebrae by vertebrae. I reached into my pocket and held onto my dental probe, mentally preparing myself for something bad to happen.

He tossed some bills onto the table.

I pushed the money aside.

"What do you want?"

"Information."

He put the bills away and I stared at him a moment. Then I saw it—a small section of hair that the turban didn't cover. I also noticed a red ketchup stain on his jacket. I hadn't noticed it at first because the jacket was red and the ketchup stain was red. A strange weird truth popped into my brain.

"I know who you are," I said

He froze for a moment evaluating the situation like a gazelle staring at a salivating tiger. Then he inhaled deeply as his hand slowly reached over to his sunglasses. He removed them, showing avocado green eyes. It then appeared as if he reached into his skin and pulled off its top layer. In reality, he was removing some kind of latex rubber mask. It was as if I were watching a caterpillar as he morphed into a beautiful butterfly—except this guy wasn't so beautiful.

A moment later, he appeared as I'd seen him many times before.

He smirked. "Hi Arnie."

Chapter Thirteen

Suddenly, my cell phone rang. It was Richard Levinsky, the PI. I thanked him for calling, but told him I'd already solved the mystery.

I stared back at the blood shot eyes and receding hairline of the man sitting in front of me. "What the hell you doing, Mickey?"

Mickey pulled off a small piece of latex that had remained stuck to his nose, rolled it into a ball and tossed it into his empty coffee mug. "I had to wear a disguise. I'm supposed to be dead."

"I know, I saw your ashes."

"Actually, that's some skin I scrapped off my leg. Always chafing. I burnt it up along with some of my old workout clothes and threw in a couple of hot dogs I ate last week. Man were they good. One hundred percent beef and no—"

"Aren't you worried someone's gonna see you here?" I asked.

"You kidding? In this dive?"

I looked around at all the drunks and realized that Mickey was probably right.

"You know you really hurt Debbie."

For the first time since I'd known him, I saw a wave of sadness pass through Mickey's face. He had always been this glib guy who never showed any trace of emotion. It had been like talking to a rock.

"I never meant to hurt her. But as time went along, I just felt something was missing from our relationship, and I didn't know how to tell her." He shrugged. "Look, I'll always love Debbie, but Stephanie is my true soul mate. We just clicked. She and I can talk on so many levels."

"I didn't realize you had more than one level."

"Hey, can you be kind here? I'm dead, you know."

"Okay, so you pretended to die to get out of marrying Debbie?"

"There's more to it than that." He pushed the plate with the remnants of his corn beef and cabbage to the side and looked at me. "Arnie, I have a bit of a problem."

I shook my head. "I'd say a lot of problems...you're childish, an ego-maniac, insensitive to other people..." I pointed to the ketchup stain on his jacket. "And worse yet, you don't send your clothes out to the dry cleaner often enough."

Mickey looked down at the stain on his jacket and tried to rub it away. "Originally, I pretended to be dead to get out of marrying Debbie, yes. I didn't see any way out. I knew I couldn't tell her about the other woman. You know how she gets."

"I guess I couldn't have expected you to be a man."

He stretched his neck, rubbed his shoulder. "You're right, I should have just told her...I couldn't."

"Well, right now she's crying her eyes out because of you." I wanted to lay it on thick, even though I knew that Debbie was questioning her whole relationship with Mickey. "Did you really blow up your dental office just to make it look like your body had been reduced to ashes?"

Mickey adjusted himself in his chair, moved close to me, and smiled as if he were going to tell me some long story with a heart-warming ending that would make everything he'd done seem okay. He'd have to be a better story-teller than John Grisham to do that.

"See, I decided to go to Vegas with Stephanie for a holiday. When we got there, I sent her to Circus Circus.

You know they have a show that runs 24 hours a day with different clowns." He spread his hands. "Big ones, small ones, some with big hats, others with baggy pants, one guy with—"

"I get the picture, lots of clowns."

"Right. Well, while she did that, I headed over to the craps tables. I played all night, sometimes winning, but at the end, I was in the hole. I had no choice but to borrow money from a couple of loan sharks."

"Mickey, you've worked as an orthodontist since dental college. Don't you have savings?"

Mickey looked down at his shoes—Gucci, I think.

His jaw began to move but no words came out at first. When the words did appear, they were whispered. "Arnie, I...I...I'm a shopaholic."

"Shopaholic?"

"Yes, I buy everything I see. You know those companies that have the late night infomercials? They wouldn't survive without me. During one spree, I must have bought twenty machines that are supposed to give you a six pack, and right now I don't even have a one pack."

"How much did you borrow?"

"Fifty grand. But here's where I screwed up..."

"So borrowing fifty grand from loan sharks wasn't where you screwed up?"

"No. The screwing up was when I left Vegas without telling them. Apparently, they like to keep tabs on people they loan money to. Crazy, eh? So when I went back to Corral, they followed me. Showed up at my door one day and told me that instead of fifty, I now owed them a hundred grand. I got angry. I told them I'm wasn't going to pay them anything cause of their nasty attitude. It turns out they don't like people saying they have a nasty attitude either. Pretty sensitive for underworld characters. I was forced into a corner and I only had one choice: make it look like I'd died. I wouldn't have to tell Debbie the truth, the gangsters would give up on me and Stephanie and I would live happily ever after. Or so I'd hoped."

I paused a moment to give my neurons a chance to regroup. "That's some story, Mickey."

"It's true. Every word of it. It sounded true didn't it?"

I thought about that one, when I noticed Mickey's eyes darting toward the door. "Oh, no," he whispered.

I turned around to look at what he had focused on— a tall, pale man with straggly blonde hair heading toward us. He wore a dark blue shirt and black pants that flared at the bottom. Bell bottoms, really? This is the kind of hip guy Mickey associates with?

As he got closer, I got this creepy vibe. His lips were frozen in a snarl and his eyes were slits. He marched slowly in a very precise way toward our table, almost zombie-like. He looked like he didn't get out too much, except maybe when he had to murder someone. It seemed to take forever, but he finally reached our table and banged on it with his fist. "Where's the guy?"

"Guy? What guy?"

"The guy that was sitting with you?"

I looked back and stared at an empty chair. Mickey had high-tailed it out of there.

Chapter Fourteen

I explained to Blondie that I had no clue who the man at my table had been. He had just come over to beg for money.

Blondie grunted and left.

Mickey was obviously involved with some dangerous characters. Was he one of Mickey's friends from Vegas? Or someone else Mickey had dissed, or maybe made their braces a little too tight? I didn't know, but I couldn't worry about that now. I had to scurry back to the office to see my first patient of the day—Randy Corcoran, a photocopy machine technician.

When I got there, I hoped to find Randy sitting in my waiting room, scared out of his wits, like everyone's supposed to be in a dental waiting room. Instead, he was kneeling in the reception area beside the spanking new photocopier, we'd nick-named, Matilda. Numerous parts lay in a big pile next to him, along with a puddle of grease.

I stared at this scene weepy-eyed as if someone had just hurt a good friend. "Randy, the cleaning and check-up was for you, not the photocopier."

"Sorry," he said, absently rubbing his narrow face and inadvertently greasing up his nose. "You were late and I had to keep my hands busy."

That's one of Randy's problems. While he easily took machines apart, he just never got around to putting them back together. I had a feeling someone would be up till the early morning with the five hundred page manual trying to make this Frankenstein Monster come alive again. I planned on it being Tanya.

I escorted Randy into my office so he couldn't get into any more mischief. I had to keep those hands busy. A few moments later, Randy sat in my dental chair, his hands grasping the arms in a death grip.

"You ready, Randy?"

"Yes, completely calm now. Don't I look calm?"

"Yes, very calm," I said, staring at his now, almost blue hands.

And those nerves of his led to his next problem— non-stop talking during dental work. On one occasion, he spent three hours trying to tell me about the physics of black holes in outer space, while he had dental dam, three cotton balls and a saliva sucker stuffed into his mouth.

Thanks to him, I have a complete knowledge of black holes, except I'm not sure if anyone would understand it when I tell them: "Eez...blll...Axr..eke."

Today's conversation went something like, and I really want to get it accurately—

"Augh...leood...mrrr...ricva...einei."

Of course, as an expert dental practitioner, I knew exactly how to translate that into English. It either meant, "You're doing a great job, Arnie," or "Are you trying to kill me?" I preferred to think he meant the first thing.

"Aigg, Errie, Sori."

"Yes, global warming is a problem, Randy."

By the time I had finished working on Randy's teeth, I believe we had discussed everything from the bad salaries of teachers to why photo-copy repairmen don't get invited to more parties. I had a few good ideas on that.

He left, promising to return to fix the copier, but I knew he wouldn't be back till next year when the cycle would repeat itself.

I had a few moments before my next patient to make a couple of notes on my current cases. I had gone wild financially and spent a buck on a new notebook. Hopefully, my accountant wouldn't find out about it.

In terms of Mickey, it seemed amazing that he wasn't dead—again. Although judging by his "new friends," that status could change at any moment. I had dealt before with people who were on the run from loan sharks and it hadn't ended well.

My problem was that I was at standstill with both my cases. I couldn't tell Debbie that Mickey was still alive. It would hurt her to know that the man she loved, had pretended to be dead so he could get out of marrying her.

Then I thought about Rodrico. Yes, I had a picture of the guy his wife hung around with, but I decided I couldn't give that to him right now. Who knows what he'd do to Judy and her companion? I didn't want that on my conscience. What the hell was I going to do?

Chapter Fifteen

The following day I trailed Judy again. I decided, however, that it was time to ramp up my investigation. I planned to accidentally run into her and pump her for information.

I found her at Joe's Fine Antiques in a small strip mall. It seemed like she went shopping a lot. I guess it relieved the stress she had from being a mob boss's wife. You know, being around all that leg-breaking could get to anyone after a while.

I parked in the tiny lot and watched as she left the antique store and entered a donut shop called 'World's Greatest Donuts.'

I figured Judy had plans to meet her sweetheart/crook/friend here. I waited and watched. A lot of people walked by looking in the window of the donut shop, but no one actually went in. The economy must be in bad shape when you can't even get people to eat the 'world's greatest donuts.'

A few moments later, he appeared.

Show time.

I sauntered into the donut emporium, intending to go right to Judy's table. However, as soon as I entered, my nasal passages were infiltrated by the sweet aromas of just-baked fritters and bear claws. I wanted one or two, or a dozen. Maybe a gallon. But, no, I had work to do. I walked swiftly past the counter, holding my breath. I slid by Judy's table, then looked back as if I had just noticed her. I slipped on my hundred-watt smile and approached, trying to avoid the enticing stares I got from the blueberry and apple donuts laying untouched on their plates.

"Hello, Mrs. Rodrico."

She looked up. Worried eyes.

"Arnie, nice to see you."

"How's everything?" I said, trying to put more wood on my smile to keep it burning.

"Fine."

She made no attempt to introduce me to her friend. So I just put my hand out to him to shake. "Hi, I'm Arnie Katz." He didn't shake it. He just gave me a look that said I should put the hand down or he was going to bring his hand up and it might end up in my face. He was a good communicator without actually using words. It sent shivers through my body. No one said anything for a moment, then Judy spoke in a subdued voice.

"Arnie, if you happen to see my husband, please don't mention I was here with this, uh, gentleman." She put her hand on my hand. "I'd be willing to pay for your silence."

"No money necessary, Mrs. Rodrico. I just need to know what's going on."

Judy slowly let out air like a basketball that had just slid under the front wheel of a four by four.

"I might be able to help," I added.

She weighed that a moment, as if the fate of the entire free world depended on her answer, then spoke. "Okay, I'll explain the situation, but I need your discretion."

The sweetheart/crook/friend raised his eyebrows. So he wasn't a wax figure after all and I wouldn't have to bring out the match to see if he melted.

Finally, words dripped out of his mouth. "I don't think this is a good idea, Judy."

"Look, Robert, Arnie's a PI. He's helped Lou out of tight jams, many times."

Robert glared at her.

"You don't have to worry. He's a good man."

"I don't like it. This could get us both killed."

"Maybe he can help." Her eyes zeroed in on me, a hopeful look filling her face.

"I'll try." I sat down and Judy leaned forward in her chair.

"This is what it is. I had kind of a strange childhood. My parents divorced when I turned seven. I lived with my mom, never knew my dad. Mom never really talked about him, and I always felt as if something was missing from my life. Everyone would say it's just because of the divorce and not knowing my father. But I felt there was more to it than that.

"Mom passed away in her thirties. That's when I came across some letters in one of her drawers. Most of them were pretty ordinary, but one was about my brother. And that puzzled me. I'd always thought I'd been an only child."

She paused a moment, as if considering that for the first time, then continued. "It turns out I did have a brother. My mom just never told me about him. Apparently, he was a trouble-maker and had been sent to an orphanage. I knew I had to meet him. I contacted all kinds of organizations and though it took months, I finally tracked him down."

She smiled, patted the man beside her on his shoulder. "Arnie, meet my brother, Robert."

So I had been right. He wasn't a love interest. I put out my hand to shake Robert's, figuring now that we knew a little more about each other, it would be like Woodstock and love and peace with him. "Nice to meet you," I said. He didn't budge. Wax figure time again.

"You shouldn't have told him, Judy. It's gonna be bad." Robert said 'bad' like it was a long word.

I piped in. "Look, I've known Mr. Rodrico a long time and, despite everything, I think he'd be very pleased that you have a brother, Judy."

She nodded. "Yes, under normal circumstances, he might, Arnie. But these aren't normal circumstances."

She pulled out a tissue from her purse and wiped her eyes. "After I met Robert, he told me about his life and my father. That's where the problem starts."

I saw Robert putting his hands into his pockets. That always makes me nervous. Was there a gun there? Or plastic explosives? Or a grenade? Perhaps, I was over-reacting and he was simply reaching for a tissue to dry off the blood he'd gotten on his fingers two weeks ago when he shot that other PI.

"See, Robert had spent a lot of time at the orphanage. Oh, the odd family had taken him in for a few weeks, but he never got adopted. Then one day, his, and my real dad, came in and re-adopted him. Turns out he didn't know he had children. My mom had kept it from him."

Judy cleared her throat. "It turns out our father is Phil Delucca, one of the bosses of the Daroga Family. Robert eventually joined that family."

I sat back in my chair, taking all this in. "Quite a story. And I do see where the problem is."

And it was a big problem. Rodrico was head of The Larotta Family which worked the south side of Corral. They had never gotten along with The Darogas, who worked the north side. If Rodrico found out about this, it could be very bad.

"Have you talked to Phil—your dad?" I asked Judy.

She shook her head. "No, not yet. He hasn't approached me either, even though Robert has told him the story. I guess he's not sure what to do or maybe he... doesn't care about me." She wiped her eyes again.

Robert moved his face close to mine, almost challenging me. "So how do we solve that, PI?" His hands were still in his pockets, hopefully, not pulling the pin on that grenade. That would really drive his sperm count down.

I told the two of them that I would think about what the next step should be.

But I really didn't have a clue what to do.

Chapter Sixteen

I decided I needed to have a rest away from all the crazy things that had happened recently. Some of my best ideas came when I just relaxed. I could have had a green tea or a nap to clear my head. But I decided to do something else.

I headed over to 'Sumatra Yoga," a small yoga studio located in the east end of Corral. From the front, it resembled every other building on the block. In the back, however, burn marks covered the bricks. A few years back when the studio first moved to the neighborhood, there were problems. 'Yogi Yoga' across the road didn't like the competition. It was quite a site to see these spiritual, peace-loving instructors tossing torches and firebombs at one another.

Eventually, it was all sorted out when the two groups had a "Yoga off" and "Yogi Yoga" lost. A truce was declared and since then, no trouble.

The owner of 'Sumatra Yoga,' Madame Yama, is a slight oriental woman who's all smile. She calls her yoga system, "Sushimi," and it combines parts of other yoga disciplines as well as her own unique ideas. Kind of like a smorgasbord without the food.

Although short, Madame Yama exudes this high-octane positive energy. It's nice to be around that kind of magic.

When she saw me, the smile plumped up three sizes larger.

"Arnie, you look great."

"Thanks," I said, not thinking that hanging around with mobsters and criminals had done my complexion any good.

"Come in, we're just starting class."

I walked into her studio and saw the other class members bent in all kinds of weird shapes that I sometimes thought the human body wasn't meant to be forced into. I sat down on one of the mats and followed her expert direction.

Soon, I was The Caterpillar and The Boll Weevil and The Preying Mantis. Mrs. Yama said I was so good that someone might try and get me with bug spray. We both had a good laugh. I left the studio feeling on top of the world. Although I have to admit she gave you one tough workout, and I wondered how the real Boll Weevils got along without a medical plan.

When I went back to the dental office, Tanya's eyes flew over my body. The first thing she said was, "Madame Yama?"

I nodded.

I looked out at the waiting room, not believing what I saw. It was empty. "Wow, great job, Tanya. You've finally mastered your overbooking problem. I had plans to send you to 'overbooking anonymous' or get you on a twelve step program, but I guess that won't be necessary now."

"No, it's not that."

"Was there a bomb scare?"

"It's the holiday weekend, remember? I just came in to clear up a few things."

I guess I'd been so busy I had forgotten all about Memorial Day. Most people were probably at their cottages. Pity. Here I was all relaxed and everything, and I didn't have enough patients to get me stressed. Oh well. I decided to sit in my office for a while and continue working on my acupressure points like Madame Yama had shown me.

I lay back in my chair and let the peaceful calm flow through my body. It had been a long time since I'd felt this good. I savoured it. I was about to press the acupressure point on my upper thigh to take me into the third stage of Kamuto—the highest level of relaxation, when the door sprang open and Tanya stood there—shoulders tensed; eyes wide open. She raised a shaky right hand toward me.

"Arnie, there's a bit of a thing going on in the waiting room."

"What? Some ghosts are arguing?" I laughed. Relaxing seemed to have made my sense of humor sharper, more insightful.

It didn't seem to calm her down much. "You take care of it, Tany," I said. "And try and relax. Think of a babbling book, a forest full of trees—their leaves swaying in the wind, back and forth, back and for—"

"Arnie, I don't think..."

"That's right, don't think. Just calm your core." I put my hand on my stomach, took in a few deep breaths.

At that moment, Debbie burst into my office, her face all red, anger in her voice. "Arnie, what the hell were you thinking?"

Relaxation gone!

Chapter Seventeen

I brought Debbie into the back room where there wasn't any expensive dental equipment to break, just in case. I piled up the boxes of toothbrushes and we sat on those.

"Calm down, Debbie. Whatever it is, it's not that big a deal."

She inhaled sharply and seemed to relax a little. She didn't look like she'd still rip my legs off. My arms maybe, just not my legs.

"What's the problem?"

"I found this at my place." She reached into her purse and pulled out my missing notebook.

"Oh great, thanks. I thought I'd lost it."

I reached out to take it from her hand. She pulled it back, riffled the pages, looking for something.

"Page ten had an interesting notation."

"Oh?"

Her finger scanned the page. Here it is. "Mickey had a girlfriend, Stephanie Warwick." Debbie looked at me daggers. "Do you remember that?"

"Uh, yeah."

"How come you didn't tell me?"

"I was just thinking on paper. I wasn't sure it was true."

"But now you are, right?"

I sighed. "Yeah."

"Now, according to the date here, that happened a few days ago. Knowing how fast you work, I'd say you saw her already. Debbie leaned back, almost falling off toothbrush mountain. "So tell me about her. What does she look like...blonde, big boobs, gorgeous?"

"Actually..." I looked at Debbie, unsure how to answer that. Knowing Debbie's ability to be a human lie detector, I decided I had to give her the truth. "Yeah, that's pretty much her."

She moved her lips around like she was trying to twist them into some kind of origami shape. "Don't you know anything about women? That's not what we want to hear. We want you to say she's ugly, has no teeth and is bald."

"Sorry."

"No wonder you and I broke up."

That hurt. But I didn't say anything. "Look she's very nice and—"

"God, you really don't know women. Couldn't you have said she was a bitch or something?"

I shook it off. "Debbie, I can't lie to you. You know me too well."

She didn't say anything for a moment. That worried me even more than when she spoke. What was building up inside of her?

"What I've learned in the PI business is that usually men and women who have affairs are decent people. No one's the bad guy like you see in the movies. It's just sometimes they let their hormones get out of control."

She rubbed the side of her head. "Did you ever cheat on me?"

I glared at her. "I think you know the answer to that."

She nodded.

Knowing how headstrong she is, I had to ask her the question. "You're not going to go see Stephanie, right? That would be bad."

"What? Oh no, no, never." Then in a quiet voice, she said, "So what other dirt do you have on Mickey?"

I sighed. I had to tell her the whole story. I didn't want to, but I figured she'd find out either by woman's intuition or by spiking my green tea with Sodium Pentothal when I wasn't looking. "Listen, I have a pretty free day today. Why don't you and I go out for a tea and talk?"

A few moments later we sat at a table in Tony's Diner, a Corral hotspot. Everyone came here for the great brunch and homey atmosphere. The waitresses were older and called everyone *hon.*

Our seats overlooked the kitchen and we could smell the scintillating aromas of eggs and bacon, done Tony style—lots of exotic spices. Maybe that would put Debbie in a better mood for what I had to tell her.

We used to come here every Friday morning and have their breakfast special. A great deal. Eggs, toast and sweet potato fries—$4.99. Tony always tried to get us to set a date for our wedding. He wanted to cater it and be best man.

We sat down at our old table with the tartan table cloth and waited to be served. I was happy for the wait, anything to take up time before telling Debbie about Mickey. A few seconds later, however, Tony stood beside us with his familiar moustached upper lip. "Hey, Arnie, Debbie." He tapped my shoulder, then kissed Debbie on both sides of her cheek. "It's so nice that you two are back together again. I've missed us."

I wasn't aware we were a threesome, but Tony evidently thought so. Debbie and I looked at one another, both feeling awkward. "Uh, Tony," I said. "We're not really back together. We're just talking."

"You can't keep true love apart." He winked. "You want the usual?"

I didn't argue about the true love thing. He didn't know any of our back story. Debbie ordered a coffee.

They were out of green tea, but I managed to rein in my outrage and order a Perrier.

I talked to Debbie about the weather, how my dental practice was going, my dad's attempts to get me into law, about how I thought I should shave my sideburns, in fact, anything my fried brain could come up with just so I wouldn't have to bring up the status of Mickey's alive-ness. I guess I just didn't know how to break it to Debbie that her boyfriend, who she thought had died in an explosion, and was apparently spending his afterlife in a jar of mayo—was still alive. "Listen, about Mickey, he, uh—"

"Before you start, I know you didn't like the guy. And you had good reason for that, but I hope you're not going to bad mouth him. Hey, he wasn't the greatest person, but he is dead."

This wasn't going to be easy. I took a big sip of my Perrier. "Actually, he's not."

"What?"

"Mickey's alive."

Her eyes grew so large I thought they'd burst.

"Alive?"

"Yes."

The color left her face and she looked like she was going to faint—or kill me.

Chapter Eighteen

"And how in the freaking world, do you know this?"

I explained to Debbie about the letter and meeting Z/Mickey at the diner.

She didn't speak for several moments—different parts of her brain probably trying to reconcile this strange new information with other parts. The sane part saying, "Don't kill this guy, his patients need him," the insane part saying, "There's lot of dentists out there."

She picked up a sharp knife and absently stabbed it in the air. It didn't make me feel any more secure. I just hoped both of us would be leaving the table alive.

In an emotionless voice she said, "Why didn't you tell me before?"

"I wasn't sure it was going to be him."

"And when did you find all this out?"

"Yesterday."

She didn't react at first, but I sensed an undercurrent of anger building. I had a hunch insane Debbie wanted to come out and do some serious damage, but sane Debbie was straining to hold her in. I hoped sane Debbie had been doing a lot of weight training. I was sure if she let insane Debbie out, the city would be destroyed like Tokyo after the well-documented Godzilla attack of 1974.

I had to be careful what I said here. "I just thought it would make you feel worse. You know, with all the stuff that you were already dealing with."

The color started to come back to her face.

"Look, it's not enough that he left you at the altar. He even blew up his office and faked his death to avoid marrying you. How bad would that have made you feel?"

"Thanks for reminding me. Now I know that I'm totally un-loveable." She pouted.

I put my arm around her. "I'm sorry, Debbie, but it is what happened. You told me you didn't want me to hide anything from you."

"Yeah, you're right. I guess I'm over-reacting. You know how I get. I'm angry for a few minutes and then I cool down."

I nodded, realizing how little self-awareness she had. "Yeah, that's you all right, quick-cool-down-Debbie."

She brushed her hair back, but I could see from her eye movements that all kinds of thoughts were flying around in her brain. It reminded me of balls being flung out from a mechanical tennis ball shooter. "Mickey did feel bad about it, didn't he?"

"Absolutely," I said, I'm sure, a little over enthusiastically. "Very upset. It was pathetic to see the man weep like that."

I stared at Debbie, trying to read her thoughts, but with her, it was almost impossible. One time she might think one thing, another time, exactly same situation, she'd think something totally different.

"The main reason Mickey said he was dead had nothing to do with you. It's because he was up to his molars in gambling debts. And apparently the people he owes money to are the type that would kill someone to get what they want."

An expression appeared on her face that I'd never seen before. Then she said something that I really didn't expect.

"That poor poor man."

Chapter Nineteen

Debbie asked me where Mickey was now. I told her the truth.

"After that guy approached us at the restaurant, Mickey ran off, and I have no clue where he is."

She nodded, seemed to accept it. I found that a bit odd since generally, Debbie didn't go with the flow.

Maybe she had matured, decided to not act so abruptly when circumstances changed. Either that, or her shell-shocked brain was working out ways of taking revenge on Mickey. Or me. Or someone else. I just hoped Humphrey, my turtle, was safe from all of this.

I drove her home and she seemed almost back to normal, even said goodbye like she wasn't going to put a bomb in my car.

I went to the office and worked on a few patients, then took a break in the backroom and tried to sort out my other case.

I had promised Judy that I wouldn't say anything to Rodrico. But I was working for the man so I felt obligated to tell him what I knew. Big conflict of interest. Of course, on the other hand, telling a mobster that his wife's brother is working with people he hates may not be a smart thing to do.

I didn't come up with much other than changing my name to Sven and moving to Sweden.

I was so deep in thought that I didn't notice the exact moment Tanya had joined me in the backroom. I looked over and watched her remove a message pad and some pens from the supply cupboard.

"Lots of messages?"

"Uh huh." She began walking out.

"From whom?"

She twisted around to face me. "The thing is last week we got a lot of new clients. I tried to book them for Tuesday, but a lot of them couldn't make it. So I had to get them in for..."

"Easy Thursday?"

"Uh huh."

"You know I think we should change the name of 'Easy Thursday.' Maybe to something like, 'the day my receptionist wants to make me crazy.'"

"I think it's too long, Arnie."

She was about to leave when she stared at me for a moment."

I stared back. "What's wrong?"

"You kinda look like you're five years old and you've come in last in the potato sack race."

"I'm just having a problem with a case I'm working on."

"You'll figure it out. You're the best PI/dentist there is." She rubbed my back.

"Thanks," I said, trying to fake a smile. Must have been pretty good; she smiled back. Unless hers was fake too.

"It's just I have some bad news I have to tell one of my clients, and he can be, uh, very vengeful."

"Well, I always think that it's your job to tell someone whatever you need to tell them. You aren't responsible for how they react. Like my Aunt Tess. Usually I go to Texas to see her in July. But last year, I had to tell her I couldn't come till November. She cried and yelled and threatened to keep the cheese grater she was going to give me as a birthday present. Can you believe that?"

I shook my head, making a mental note to contact *Ripley's Believe it or Not.*

"It wasn't pretty, but it was just something I had to do." Tanya put her foot on a box of Dental Dam like she had won WWII single handedly.

She did have a point. It was my job to tell Rodrico the bad news. Of course, the difference was that I didn't think Aunt Tess had murdered too many people with her cheese grater. Not that I was sure about that.

We both left the back room and I finished up the rest of my patients. I headed home, not having any new brainstorms about what to do about anything.

I fed Humphrey and told him I missed him. No reaction. He just stared, then finished off the tiny piece of meat in the corner of his terrarium. I have a hunch he's emotionally stunted.

The next morning when I awoke, the brainstorm I'd been waiting for had arrived. I now had a plan for Judy and Robert. It required lots of confidence so to get extra mental power, I had an extra cup of green tea.

Twenty minutes later, I had driven to the house on Dunkirk that I'd seen Robert enter. The door opened and Phil Chimera, the boss of The Daroga Mob Family stood in front of me—his porkpie hat low on his head. I pressed an acupressure point to relax. I hoped it was the right one.

"What do you want?" He didn't actually pronounce those words, more like grunted them out. With that kind of attitude, I bet he didn't get too many people wanting to join the mob during their membership drives.

"I'd like to see Robert."

"He know you?"

"Yeah."

He went inside the house and a few moments later, Robert appeared at the door, wearing a black sports jacket and black tie. His hair combed back perfectly like last time. "What are you doing here?"

"I've been thinking about your, uh, situation, and I believe I've found a way of resolving things."

Robert stared at me for a moment, like he was a psychiatrist staring at his new patient who happens to bark like a dog.

A moment later, he opened the door and ambled outside. We walked through the front yard to the side of the house where groups of lilacs were blossoming. I breathed in the scintillating aroma and explained what my plan entailed. He didn't seem that keen on it.

"That's the worst idea I ever heard, man."

"It's our only chance."

"I don't like it. Too many variables, chances for things to go wrong."

It seemed like it was a no go. But then I phoned Judy and discussed it with her. She liked the plan and convinced Robert to go along with it.

An hour later, Robert, Phil and I stood in front of Rodrico's door.

Phil looked nervous. He kept rubbing his hands together, like he was trying to start a fire. It felt surreal to see a mobster like that. Usually, you thought of these guys as invincible.

The door opened. Rodrico appeared, his eyes doing a crazy dance. It's as if Scarface showed up on his front step with a clear complexion..

"You're outta your territory, Phil."

"We gotta talk."

"Is this a trick?"

Phil shook his head. "No."

Rodrico stood for a moment, not moving, like he had turned into a block of granite. A moment later, he nodded, told us to come in. We all sat down at the dining room table. I looked around the room and I gotta admit the tableau reminded me of that painting, *The Last Supper*. Except with gangsters.

I just hoped it wouldn't be my "last supper."

Judy, wearing a black evening gown and white pumps, sauntered down the stairs and joined us at the table. I noticed everyone watching her, except Phil. He had his eyes glued on Rodrico. Of course, Rodrico had his eyes glued on Phil. That's a lot of eye glue.

I held a chair out for Judy and she sat down. It was quite a gathering. Two mob bosses who hated each other, one of the mob boss's sons, the wife of a mob boss and me—a DDS.

Phil and Rodrico continued to stare at one another. A tense situation. It was like being near a nuclear reactor. You were pretty sure it was safe, but you wouldn't want to light up an El Producto.

Phil spoke. "I know we've been at odds for a long time, Lou, but maybe it's time we come together."

"Why would we do that? We ain't never gotten along."

"There was a time we did. Maybe we can go back to those days."

Rodrico shrugged. "I don't think so."

Robert glared at me. "I told you this was stupid. He ain't never gonna go for it."

Phil took a deep breath, stood, about to leave.

I jumped up. "Please stay, Phil. We have to tell him what's happened."

Rodrico froze. "Tell me what?"

Everyone stared at everyone else, no one wanting to say anything. Finally, I broke the silence. "You know you asked me to follow Judy."

"Uh huh."

"I did. And I found her with another man."

He looked over at Judy, outraged. "I knew it."

"But it's not what you think. That man...is her brother. And Phil is...her father."

"What?"

Judy nodded. "It's true, Lou. I've been searching for Robert for years. Finally found him." She touched Robert on his shoulder. "Then I discovered that Phil is my birth father."

Rodrico gave her a hardened stare that I'd seen once before. I believe it was just before he ordered a couple of his trusted employees be whacked.

I hoped this turned out better.

Chapter Twenty

Phil leaned over to Rodrico. "Look, Lou, this changes things. I don't want no more fights between us. Maybe we can work together, not have any more north side or south side. Just one organization. What do you say?"

Rodrico thought a moment, then got up and paced.

Phil continued. "Arnie helped me come up with a list of ways we can compromise." He pulled out the sheet of paper I'd written ideas on and handed it to Rodrico.

Rodrico read the sheet, then gazed up at his wife and her newly-found sibling. He nodded. "Maybe we can, Phil. Maybe we can." He reached out his hand to Phil and the two men shook. If there were any paparazzi within two hundred square meters who had their life insurance paid up, it would have been a Kodak moment.

"There's one more thing I need to do, Lou." Phil marched over to Judy, rubbed his hands together again, said, "Hi."

Judy grinned, a little girl grin. "Hi."

"Sorry, about, uh, everything."

"You have nothing to be sorry about. Mom never told you anything. How would you know?"

Phil nodded. "I'd like for us to talk sometime and, uh, have a—you know—relationship. But, I'm not really too good at these things."

"I'd like that."

Judy hugged Phil.

A few moments later, everyone talked liked we were all at a Christmas party with best friends.

Rodrico paid me for finding out that Judy wasn't having an affair. He even gave me a bonus. I felt great. I had brought two warring mob organizations together and helped reunite a family. Now that's a good day!

Rodrico told me to call him anytime I needed to hide a body.

Chapter Twenty-One

I got home and took out a small piece of sirloin from the fridge and dropped it into Humphrey's terrarium. He grabbed it like he was a great white shark and in two seconds the meat was gone. I had tried giving him ordinary hamburger but his head wouldn't even come out of its shell. He had high standards for a fresh water turtle living in a rent-controlled apartment.

I noticed that the answering machine light was on and I pressed the button to hear the messages.

"Son, I need you. It's an emergency."

I couldn't believe it. My dad had called.

I called his number, but got a busy signal. Although, we hadn't spoken in a long time and weren't on the best of terms, he was still my dad. I had to drive over to his place.

My dad lived in a small place off Leonard Blvd. It was an older house with faded red bricks and a silver veranda that had peeling paint. My dad had been a lawyer and could easily afford to do renovations, but his thinking was that you only fix it up when you plan to sell it.

Dad always kept the front window open. He said it gave him an opportunity to breath in the fresh air. Although, the real reason was so he could spit when he wanted—which was pretty well most of the time. I thought he would have closed the window since that incident with the postman.

I parked the car and headed toward the front door when dad appeared outside like a genii from a lamp. Knowing dad, I didn't think he'd grant me any wishes.

From first appearances, he didn't seem as if he was suffering the trauma of any emergency. He stood there, calmly smoking his Cohiba cigar, looking fantastic. Even at seventy, he had matinee idol looks, and a full head of wavy brown hair that the ladies adored. He looked better than me and he smoked and drank like a fish.

I rushed toward him. "Hey, Dad. What's up?"

He removed the cigar from his mouth and stared at me like he didn't know what I was talking about.

"You said there was an emergency."

"Oh, right, right. Come on in, you'll see what I mean."

He walked inside, I followed, preparing myself for the worst. The interior of the house looked as always, like it had been furnished by the dollar store. Cheap paintings on the wall, cheap carpet on the floor, and cheap plastic vinyl table cloth on the dining room table. Around the table were four men and in the middle of said table, a pile of poker chips.

"I don't see what you mean yet, Dad. The table isn't on fire, there are no floods and unless it's happening in the kitchen, I don't see any locusts."

He puffed on his cigar. "Aren't you happy to see your dad?"

"I just want to find out what the emergency is, that's all."

He pointed toward the table.

I looked at him, not getting it.

"We need a fifth for our poker game."

I stared at him, not believing this. "That's your emergency? That's why you wanted me here?"

"Yeah, if we don't have a fifth, the game is nowhere near as exciting. Right guys?"

I heard assorted voices say, "Uh huh," "Yeah," and "You got that right."

I threw up my hands.

"Let me introduce you to everyone, Arnie." He pointed to a fat man smoking a pipe. "That's Irv. He's a lawyer at Wilson and Associates." Irv was wearing the loudest shirt I'd ever seen—every possible shade of red and purple. He should have been in a parade. Maybe as a float. Irv grinned at me and tossed a chip into the pot.

"That's Andy and Carl." My dad indicated the two thin men wearing Armani suits sitting beside Irv. "They're brothers." Both nodded in unison like they were a synchronized poker team. They're Corral's highest paid criminal attorneys."

"Nice to meet you, guys, but I should go."

Dad gave me a disappointed look. It was the same look I received when at two years old, I failed to say the word, "money" and spit up instead.

"Come on, Son. Stay for the game. We got lots of snacks." He went to the cupboard and pulled out bags of jelly beans, Jujubes and chocolate. Did dad even know I was a dentist?

I couldn't believe the emergency was that he needed another player. The truth is I felt sorry for him. Without mom, he was lost. I made an executive decision and sat down beside Irv. I didn't play poker much, so I was surprised that I won the first hand.

Dad beamed, even wrapped his arms around me. "Great job, Son."

That got me suspicious. Dad never complimented me on anything. And the last time he hugged me was when he performed the Heimlich manoeuvre.

"What's going on here, Dad?"

Dad looked at me and I could see his mind working out what he should tell me—-the whole truth and nothing but the truth or truth-light. "Alright, Son. It's an intervention."

"What do you mean, an intervention?"

Irv put his arm on my shoulder. "It's about your choice of career, Arnie. Your dad feels that you must have been on drugs if you went into dentistry rather than become a lawyer. Especially, with your dad's contacts."

I turned to my dad. "I've told you a hundred times, I'm happy being a dentist."

"Then why are you acting crazy and working as a private detective too."

"It's a hobby."

"A dangerous hobby. You could get killed."

"I'm very careful."

"Plus, you know dentistry has the highest rate of depression. Not to mention suicide. Between that and your being a private eye, you're really cutting down your lifespan." He moved his thumb and finger close together to show how much I was cutting it down.

I'd had it. This wasn't the first time Dad had tried to get me to switch careers. "Look, Dad, I made my choice. That's it." I got up from my chair. "I gotta go."

As I headed toward my car, I passed the open window and heard Irv say, "Drugs, definitely, drugs."

Chapter Twenty-Two

After the incident with Dad, I went for a bit of a drive to get rid of some steam, then headed back to my office to take care of some afternoon appointments. Usually, Tanya got all tensed up by about two, what with her eight coffees, overflowing waiting room, and a DDS who was out of the office more than he was in. But today she seemed calm.

"What's up?" I asked.

"Nothing," she said. "Everything's great."

My forehead crinkled. "Who is this person? Everything is never great."

"It's just the way I'm feeling."

More crinkles. Either she had a drug habit, gotten her nose into some of the laughing gas, or she was dating someone new. Since she never took so much as an aspirin and didn't like laughing all that much, I cleverly deduced the latter. But, of course, knowing Tanya's dating history I was concerned.

"You're seeing someone aren't you?"

She giggled, seemed almost drunk. I wasn't giving up the idea of the laughing gas just yet.

"I've been going out with that guy I met at Debbie's wedding."

"Mr. Hair Weave?"

"He doesn't have a hairweave. It's real."

"A real hairweave?"

She rolled her eyes. "Very funny."

"What's he do?"

"Real Estate for celebrities and CEOs of companies. You should hear about the house he lives in. Eight thousand square feet. There's a hot tub, a sauna, a pool, seven rooms."

"Where is it?"

"The Hollywood Hills. Next to Robert Livingston's place."

"Robert Livingston?"

"Yeah, he's the guy who was in that show *Wild Fever*. You know, the one where each week..."

"Yeah, I remember. In the jungle. Like Tarzan. Didn't Livingston have a hairweave too?"

"Forget the hairweave. I think I've found my 'Mr. Right,' Arnie. Aren't you happy for me?"

Tanya found a 'Mr. Right' every month or so, only they usually turned out to be 'Mr. no-commitment,' 'Mr. take her money and run,' or 'Mr. bank robber, but good person.' I usually kept my mouth closed, but this time it looked like she really loved the guy. I had to say something.

"Sure, I'm happy for you, Tanya. It's just...have you been to the house?"

"No, not yet."

"How long you been going out?"

"A few weeks."

"Have you met any of his friends?"

"No, but..." Suddenly, her eyes got all squinty. "Hey, don't PI me, Arnie."

"I'm sorry, Tany. I just want you to be careful."

"I appreciate it. But I know he's telling the truth."

"I hope so, honey."

"Tonight we're going to The Golden Root, that fancy new Thai restaurant that opened up in Corral. The one where you cook your own meat."

"Sounds like what I want when I go out. To cook my own food. Do they make you do the dishes too?"

She good-naturedly hit me on the back. "Anyway, it'll be nice to have some excitement. It's been pretty quiet around here lately, eh?"

"Yeah. Very quiet." I didn't want to tell her that I had just spent the afternoon with a man who could have my ears ripped off and used as Christmas ornaments.

I went home and had my usual oatmeal before bed, then flossed up a storm while listening to Mozart's Fifth. I find the rhythmic nature of music helps make flossing much more efficient. Although I'm not sure Mozart would have been pleased having 'flossing music' as his legacy.

I went to bed, drifted into a deep sleep. But during the night, someone buzzed my apartment door. I checked the clock beside my bed—three in the morning. I figured it was Gino. I buzzed him up

A moment later, I opened the door and saw a wide smile beaming in my direction—Debbie's. She marched in, gave me a sensual kiss, then pushed me onto the bed.

"Debbie, what are you doing?"

The smile stayed plastered on her face like someone had shellacked it there. "I missed you."

"We've been over this, remember? Besides, you've moved on and I've moved on."

"But you haven't moved on. You're still single, not going out with anyone."

I felt my eyebrows rise. "How do you know that?"

"I did some research."

"Research?"

"I talked to Tanya."

I shook my head. "She doesn't know everything that goes on in my life."

"She says she does."

Actually, Debbie was probably right on that one. Tanya probably knew more about my life than I did. If I was ever asked to write my autobiography, I'd have her do it.

"Look, I'm not going out either. My husband to be is dead"

"He's not dead."

"I meant, dead to me."

"Oh, right."

She kissed my chin, then slid her lips little by little onto my lips. Soft kisses. Warm kisses. They felt good. Like the old days when we were back at college.

Then like a jazz musician, she improvised by kissing my cheeks, my forehead, my ears. I began to think that maybe, just maybe, she and I should get back together.

She took her mouth away from my face and spoke. "I love you, Arnie. Always did. I just got sidetracked along the way."

My brain swirled with the sweet memories of when we first met.

"Let's try again."

I looked deeply into her eyes. "Are you sure?"

"Yes, I'm sure."

I moved my face closer to hers. I puckered up my lips about to give her the best darn kiss she ever had.

A knock at the door.

She stared at my lips. "Don't answer it, Arnie. There'll be other people at your door in the future. You can answer those."

"I have to. It could be the landlord telling me there's a fire next door."

She grabbed my arm tight. "There's no flames coming through the wall yet. We've still got time." She moved her lips closer to mine.

I moved away. "Debbie, I have..."

"Humphrey would alert you if there was a fire."

I ignored that and walked toward the door. When I opened it, I was shocked to see two policemen—one tall, one short.

The tall one spoke. "Hello, sir. We've tracked a Debbie Walters to this address. Is she here?"

"Debbie? What's this about?"

The tall officer turned to her. "Are you Miss Walters?"

She looked at me, worried, then at the cops. "Yes."

I didn't know what was happening. One minute we're messing around and the next, the police are here looking for Debbie. Maybe messing around is against the law in this part of Corral.

The tall cop spoke. "Stephanie Warwick was murdered last night."

My jaw dropped.

"Fingerprints were found at the scene and they belonged to Debbie Walters."

Chapter Twenty-Three

Debbie accompanied the officers down to 53 Division. I called my lawyer, Bob Lanker, and had him meet me there.

After forty minutes of questioning, Debbie left the interrogation room looking pale and confused. If Bob hadn't been with her, I had a hunch she would have confessed to stealing the secret recipe for Kentucky Fried Chicken.

Bob put his hand on my shoulder. "Sorry, Arnie. Did what I could. But they feel they have a strong case."

"Strong case? How? You just have to talk to Debbie to know she wouldn't kill anyone."

"I understand how you feel. But I've defended people who seemed completely innocent but turned out to have committed the most heinous crimes."

I glared at Bob. "Thanks for the support."

"Just the way it is, Arnie." He shrugged and left. I went to talk to Debbie.

Normally, I wouldn't have been able to speak to her so soon, but I knew a couple of higher-ups at the force.

They took me to one of those rooms where you talk to the prisoners through a glass partition. Beside me sat a guy with a three-day-old beard and numerous facial scars. He looked like he should be on the other side of the glass.

I picked up my phone.

"Hey, Debbie."

She didn't move, just stared at something in the distance, almost comatose. I knocked on the glass. She blinked a few times and seemed to return to earth, then picked up her phone. I forced a smile onto my face, but she didn't give one back. "You okay?"

"Yeah, yeah. Just tired."

I knew I had to get it out of the way. "So you went to see Stephanie last night?"

Blank stare. "Uh huh."

"Didn't I tell you not to go?"

"I don't recall."

"Debbie, when we were going out, you remembered everything—including the number of the guy at the factory who inspected the socks you got me for Christmas."

"X64950W?"

"Yeah. So I think you might remember me telling you not to go see Stephanie."

She rubbed her forehead. "I had to know what she looked like."

"I told you."

"I had to see for myself. She stole Mickey from me."

I rolled my eyes, exasperated. "You told me you were over Mickey."

"I am over Mickey. It's the principle. She stole something that belonged to me. Even if I didn't still want him. You know, like you're happy to donate a dress to charity, but when they come to actually pick it up, you have second thoughts."

"That's not the same thing at all." I shot a glance at Mr. Criminal beside me. He gave me a full mouth smile, showing four teeth in the front. I took out my dental business card and gave it to him.

Debbie leaned forward, almost pleading. "I didn't kill her, Arnie. We just had a nice chat, that's all."

"You told her about you and Mickey?"

She paused, seeming to gather her thoughts. "Not exactly."

"What exactly did you say?"

"That I, uh, work with you."

I rolled my eyes. "We don't work together."

"She remembered you, by the way. Said you were nice."

"Great. What else did you talk about?"

"Just that you and I were investigating Mickey's case."

"And then you left?"

"First I asked her a few simple questions."

"Like what?"

She shrugged. "Just some questions."

I gave her the stare that got murderers to confess. It also worked well at Gimley's department store when I took back that crockpot even though they had a no return policy.

"Okay, I asked her if she was in love with Mickey."

"Uh huh. And she said?"

Debbie took a few breaths, then looked down, like she was a six year old who just lost her puppy. "Yes."

"Then you went straight home?"

"Almost. I, uh, may have talked to a few neighbors, hung around the halls. Maybe the super accused me of stalking...you'll get me out of here, right, Arnie?"

I had no clue, but I had to at least seem positive for Debbie's sake. "Yeah, of course, it just may take a bit of time."

"Thanks." She leaned forward to kiss me, but her lips ended planted on the glass partition. I'm not sure she found it all that satisfying.

As I left, feeling bad that I had given her reason for hope where none may exist, I noticed that Mr. Criminal beside me, was using my business card to floss his teeth.

Chapter Twenty-Four

I walked down the hall of the police station and stopped at Rick Madison's office. He was one of those higher-ups I knew. The chief.

I entered the door of his always messy office. Today, the files and crumbled sheets of paper seemed to cover every inch of his desk. Various chairs had piles of folders stacked on them and in the corner there were numerous half-torn boxes. On the floor in front of his desk were broken pieces of surveillance equipment crowded together in a kind of 'village of the damned.'

Rick sat at his desk reading a file.

He raised his head to greet me and I could see he hadn't changed one iota. Of course I've never figured out what an iota is. But his looked pretty much the same.

He still had pock-marked skin from early bad acne, a balding head that cast a shadow on the wall that resembled, coincidentally enough, a bald eagle, and a bloated body, probably by too much drink, and maybe too little of anything remotely healthy. To him, grease was a vegetable. I have a hunch if he ever cried, bourbon tears would flood down his cheeks.

I liked Rick, if not just because, next to him, I was a Greek Adonis.

"What do you want, Katz? You still owe me a dinner for getting that license plate info on the Watkin's case."

"I took you out to dinner."

"You call Taco Bell dinner? And why wasn't dessert included? Dessert at Taco Bell costs 97 cents. You have to be some kind of cheapskate to not pay for a Carmel Apple Empanada."

"I was thinking of you. It's bad for your complexion. You've got to keep up those swarthy good looks."

"Right. Always thinking of me."

I looked over at the corkboard on the wall. It had a wanted poster for the 'Orthodontist Killer' with a sketch of what he looked like. "Any movement on the case?"

"We have a possible suspect."

"That's great news."

Rick moved his head from side to side as if he was unsure it was great news. Either that or he had springs holding his head in place and they needed to be replaced. "We'll see. I'm sure you didn't come all this way to chit chat. What do you want?"

"Do you know anything about the Debbie Walters case?"

"The woman who murdered Stephanie Warwick?"

"She didn't murder her, but yeah."

"You know her?"

"Old girlfriend."

He rubbed his chin, as if that changed everything. "Well, we have two theories. One is that when she found out her fiancée, Mickey Harrison, had gotten involved with this Stephanie woman, she flew into a jealous rage, drove over there and shot her."

"She wouldn't do that."

He shrugged.

"What's the other theory?"

He paused a moment before speaking. "A possible suspect in the 'Orthodontist' killings that I just mentioned."

My mouth flew open as if there were strings attached and I was on some big puppet stage. "You think she's the Orthodontist Killer?"

"I'm afraid so."

"No way. Stephanie Warwick was an actress, not an orthodontist.

Rick stood up quickly as if someone had dangled a porterhouse in front of him. "Yes, she used to be an actress, but then the work dried up and she went back to school to become—wait for it—an orthodontist."

I shook my head in disbelief, wondering why Stephanie hadn't mentioned that to me. "But the other orthodontists who got hit were established professionals."

Rick swished his mouth around as if he'd just tasted a bad Apple-Brown Betty, then walked around to the front of his desk. "You know, it's funny, but usually murderers don't care that much about being consistent."

"You don't actually believe Debbie killed Stephanie."

"I don't know what to believe right now."

I didn't like it, but I did understand his position. The Mayor of Corral was probably breathing down his neck to get the Orthodontist killer case solved. And right now, the closest thing he had to a suspect was Debbie. He had to hold onto her. Still, surely he could tell just by talking to her that she couldn't kill anyone. She got teary-eyed eating the bacteria in yogurt.

I pointed to the picture of the male figure in the trench coat on the Orthodontist Killer wanted poster. "Debbie's a woman, in case you haven't noticed."

"That's just a description from one person who claimed to have seen someone suspicious leaving the office of one of the orthodontists who was killed. It could be completely wrong." He rubbed his chin again. "Look, Arn, seeing how it's your girlfriend—"

"Ex-girlfriend."

"Right, ex-girlfriend. I'll see what I can do. But, no promises."

"Appreciate it."

"Appreciate, as in dinner?"

I nodded. "Yeah, sure."

"Dessert this time? You must have made 97 cents since our last meal together."

I let out a glimmer of a smile as I walked out of his office. Although, I had to admit, I felt more depressed than when I went in.

Chapter Twenty-Five

I decided to go to Stephanie Warwick's funeral for two reasons—one to pay my respects. I did meet her and she seemed like a good person. Two—to see if I could make some contacts who might help me solve her death and get Debbie out of jail.

Personally, I hate funerals. They always make me feel sad. So I looked forward to this one about as much as eating my own lasagne. (It's not that bad if you don't mind lasagne that requires the use of an electric cutting tool to slice it.)

What made it worse was the spooky day. A mixture of dark clouds, rain, lightning. It reminded me of every horror movie that I'd seen as a child. The dashing hero ends up at a local cemetery fighting with a werewolf. Hopefully, that wolf fellow would be somewhere else today, maybe getting a shave and some anger management therapy.

I drove to the Leamington Arch Cemetery for the eleven o'clock services. I stopped off at a local café and drank a cup of green tea. After that, I felt ready to take on the world or at least that dry cleaner who said the stain was there when I brought the pants in.

At the cemetery, I saw a small group of people standing near a tombstone. I only counted six and didn't see Mickey. He said that Stephanie had been the love of his life, so where was he?

I walked over to the group and saw the casket lying on the ground. The six people standing around were mostly older—sixty to seventy. They all seemed to be looking everywhere except the casket. I guess none of us wants to think about death—even at a funeral.

Lightning bolts crashed the dark sky. Ribbons of rain poured down. Scary enough, but then I felt a tap on my shoulder. I jumped, upset that I hadn't filled my pockets with wolfs bane before I'd come.

I turned to see that the tap-per was not a monster created by Universal Studios, but instead a tall distinguished grey-haired man with small, sad eyes.

"Hi, I'm Stephanie's grandfather, Maurice Saiton. That's Saiton—S-a-i-t-o-n. I always spell it so people don't get the wrong idea."

I nodded.

"I just wanted to meet the people who've braved the weather and come to see Stephanie before she takes that final journey."

I shook his hand. "Arnie Katz. I'm...uh, was, a, uh, friend."

"She had lots of those...at least that's what I thought." He pointed to the five other people who had come to pay their respects.

"Maybe it's the weather."

He tilted his head to one side, thinking. He looked about seventy and I worried he might tip over, so I moved my head the other way to counter balance.

"I just hope we can find out who did this. Personally, I think it's the creepy guy she used to hang around with."

There were lots of creepy guys involved in this case. He'd have to do better than that. One came to me instantly. "Mickey?"

"Who's Mickey?"

"Ah, just a name I heard."

"No, I'm talking about Daniel Richards."

"Who's he?" I asked.

"Last time I spoke to Stephanie, she said they were involved."

Involved? How can that be? Mickey said she was his soul mate. He was going to marry her. Was she two-timing him?

"Apparently, he's an antiquities dealer. The police have cleared him, though. They say they have their suspect, some young woman."

I gulped.

"But I saw the woman," he added, "and I really can't see her killing Stephanie, no matter what the circumstances."

At least Debbie had another person in her corner. "So this Daniel guy, where does he work?"

"Some place on Jurston Street, I believe." His sad eyes looked deeply into mine. "Listen, Arnie, I know we've just met, but I wondered if you would be kind enough to be one of the pallbearers. I thought there'd be more people here today. And some of them look too old to be carrying a casket."

I didn't have to think about it. "Sure."

Chapter Twenty-Six

The only address for Daniel Richards, Antiquities Dealer, was 175 Jurston Ave. Oddly enough, it belonged to an apartment building, a run-down one at that. I found Daniel Richards's name on the list outside, but decided not to buzz. Sometimes it's more fun to surprise people.

The apartment building door was locked so I waited until somebody left. That person turned out to be an elderly woman with a cane. I snuck inside as if I lived there. If anyone had stopped me, I would have said I lived in 806. Of course, it could turn out that they knew the guy in 806 or, even worse, the woman in 806. But I had a plan for that too. I called it 'the getting the hell out of there,' plan.

I boarded an empty elevator which seemed to go snail-slow. It had been wall-papered with pictures of rockets as if that would make it seem like it was going faster. Didn't work.

We stopped at floor three and an odd-looking guy with a scar joined the party. Every few moments, he'd stare at me, with this creepy look. Now I know how Humphrey feels when I watch him sunning in his terrarium.

The elevator landed with a thud on the eighth floor. I got out, surprised by how dark the hall was. I figured the super had that idea. That way you wouldn't notice the mouldy carpet and graffiti on the walls so much.

I walked down the hall to Daniel's apartment and knocked. I heard nothing for a moment, then a scrambling sound like a big hamster padding across a newspaper.

I heard, "Yes?" behind the peephole. If a hamster could speak, these were the squeak-like sounds he'd make.

"Daniel?"

"Uh huh."

"I'm investigating the death of Stephanie Warwick. Could we talk?"

A pause, then, "You a cop?"

I shook my head, exaggerating it so that he could see it through the tiny hole. Of course, if someone passed by, they might have thought I had some weird neurological disorder. "I'm a PI." I pulled out my ID and showed it through the peephole.

"Any reason I should talk to you?"

"Depends if you're interested in helping me find Stephanie's killer."

A long silence as if his mind had gone on a holiday to Yemen. Then I heard the clicks of what sounded like seven hundred door locks being opened. I guess Daniel liked his privacy. Maybe he had lots of food pellets and a large wheel he wanted to keep to himself.

When the door opened, I saw the man of the hour, Daniel Richards. And I have to say that even though my expectations had been built up by the incredible apartment building, I was even less impressed, if that's possible, by Daniel himself.

He had a stooped posture like all the troubles of his life weighed him down and a lean, chalky-white face. He looked to be in his thirties, but the posture made him seem older. He had long black hair tied in a pony-tail at the back and wore a green shirt two sizes too big. Baggy pants that looked shiny from too many washings completed the look, making me think he probably didn't work part-time as a fashion model.

His apartment was small. And listen, I hate to continue the hamster analogy but it looked like a larger version of a hamster cage. You know, with exercise equipment in one corner and a pile of his belongings packed together in another. Newspapers were everywhere. He didn't tell me where to sit. He didn't have to. There was only one chair. It didn't seem as if he had too many guests as I had to blow dust off it. He sat down on some of the scattered newspapers.

I gave him a bright smile. "Nice place."

He blinked a few times, scratched himself in his lower left quadrant. I guess he felt we were that close that he could do it in front of me. I wasn't quite there yet.

"I loved Stephanie."

"That explains why you weren't at her funeral."

He looked away for a moment, then back at me. "It's just...I couldn't." He seemed to be on the verge of tearing up. "I was too sad."

I decided to talk about something else. Changing the subject during an emotional moment is an old PI trick. It catches the subjects off guard, sometimes getting them to reveal more than they want to. "So what exactly do you do for a living?"

"Mainly, I deal in antiquities. People come to me with valuables, either objects they've found or ones that have been left to them by departed family members. I try to broker a dealer between them and a buyer."

I looked around the pretty-much empty room. "You're doing well."

"Actually, I used to. But there were problems."

Bingo. "Are you working now?"

He nodded very enthusiastically.

"Antiquities?"

"Part-time. I had to take another job."

"And you're now king of a small country?"

He didn't crack a smile, looked down at the ground.

"Short order cook." He shrugged. "All I could get."

"Stephanie know about the job switch?"

"Actually, we were on the verge of breaking up."

"Why?"

He started rubbing his elbow, like he was trying to shine up his shirt to match the pants.

"I noticed her hanging around with some tough characters. I didn't like it. We had a lot of arguments about that. Finally, I told her that either she straighten up or I'd leave." He touched his eyes as if to stop a tear before it started. The most emotional antiquities dealer in the world. Pretty soon, I'd need a life jacket.

"When did that happen?"

"Last week."

The tear could not be stopped. It rolled down his cheek and then angled slightly and ended up on his chin. He wiped it like it was his worst enemy.

"Do you know who these people were?"

He shook his head. "Usually, I saw a short fat man. One time when I came to pick up Steph, he was just leaving. He gave me a mean look. He didn't say anything, but I got the impression he would have been happier if I wasn't there.

I asked her about him and she said they were working on something that could make millions. She'd never tell me anything more. I did notice that since she got involved with this guy, she started to dress better, had a different attitude."

"How?"

"I don't know. Not as kind. That's what I liked about her when we first met. She was sweet, understanding. But gradually she started to change. She also seemed much more interested in my antiquities business. Asked me tons of questions about it. That's the odd thing, when we first met she couldn't care less."

Change the subject time. "Where were you the night she was murdered?"

"Here." Then his face scrunched up as if there were something scary in front of him like a monster or a democrat. "You're just like the cops, you don't believe me either, do you?"

I didn't. When someone tells me that I don't believe them, it's usually not a good sign.

Chapter Twenty-Seven

I left the hamster pad, then called Rick at the police station and asked if he had any info on a Daniel Richards. He said he'd check it out and get back to me.

I had just started my car when Daniel raced out the doors of his apartment building. He carried a large plastic bag.

When he got into his 1972 Oldsmobile with the dents, I followed. His car was so rusty you could see through parts of it. Reminded me of most of Pamela Anderson's outfits.

He drove at a steady pace and didn't make any stops. We passed a lot of fast food places and my stomach told me I was hungry. But I stopped listening to it since it told me to eat those four cream puffs and I had to have my pants let out.

We ended up at Stephanie's apartment building. Lucky me, the elevator didn't work, so I had to follow him up the three flights of stairs, trying to keep the death gasps to myself.

I stayed back as much as I could and still keep track of him. He walked onto the third floor, carrying his bag. So I entered the third floor as well. He looked around for a moment as if he was pondering the meaning of life, then a few seconds later, it looked like he'd nailed it. He looked forward again, but didn't make any movements for some reason. Then I saw why, a man wearing some kind of uniform was examining the door of one of the apartments. I had a hunch it might be Stephanie's.

I stayed motionless in front of the wall, trying to blend in like a chameleon. But despite using all my mental strength to will my brown sports jacket to match the ugly-green paint on the wall, it wouldn't. I guess it had standards.

A moment later, I saw uniform-man walk away, and Daniel continue down the hall. When he reached Stephanie's door, he took out a key, opened it and walked in. I sauntered down the hallway to the door. Apparently, the police had removed the yellow, 'do not enter' tape.

Daniel had left the door open. Sloppy. I guess he'd been in a hurry to get whatever he came for.

I walked in and watched as he frantically threw various items around the apartment.

"Hey, Dan, long time no speak. Everything good?"

He stopped what he was doing and turned to me, his face, red. "What the hell you doing here?"

"I missed you. I thought we bonded."

He threw his hands in the air like they were defective and he was trying to get rid of them. "Get out."

"Just curious why you're here."

His hands drifted down toward his side. "I just came to get something I gave Stephanie."

"And that would be?"

"It doesn't matter. It's not here anyway. The police or some crook took it."

"You didn't answer the question."

I hoped he didn't tear up again. I was already emotionally spent.

"I gave her a small sculpture; now it's gone and I'm doomed." His face turned morose and he kicked one of the shelves. Clear the building, I sensed more waterworks.

"Do you mind if I check your bag?"

He threw it to me.

"There's nothing there, it's empty—like my life."

I felt the bag and realized he'd told the truth. Probably on both accounts.

He headed toward the door. "I'm going."

I let him leave. He hadn't committed any crime and I probably wouldn't get any more information out of him today. "Keep in touch."

He didn't say anything, just scowled, then left.

I took a few moments to examine Stephanie's apartment. I looked at the shelf that I had examined last time. Two of the objects were still there, but one was missing. It was the bracelet with the tiny figures. Is that what he had been searching for? I decided to go after him and ask him that very question when I heard a scuffing sound in the hall. I stayed still for a moment listening. Had Daniel come back with a gun? Or his gang of fellow hamsters? The door slowly opened. I held my breath, and my periodontal extractor.

Chapter Twenty-Eight

The first thing I noticed was the smile. Wide, angelic, full of good nature. Next, the waist-long brown hair and the nails. They were a 'glow in the dark' shade of orange.

"May I ask who you are?" she said in a sing-songy voice.

I didn't do sing-songy. Once, at a karaoke bar, I sung a few bars of *Love Me Tender*—Elvis style, and the female m.c. told me to take it outside. Personally, I think my swivelling hips just got her too hot.

So instead of singing any greetings, I dug down deep and brought my most charming smile out of moth balls. I didn't want to frighten her so I only turned it up half blast. "I'm a PI looking into the death of Stephanie Warwick."

Relief spread over her face. "I'm glad someone's looking into it. I'm Angela, by the way, Stephanie's next door neighbour." She looked around the room like a depressed bee in the desert who hadn't been able to find a flower to pollinate.

"I miss her." She paused for a moment as if trying to hold back tears. "Anything I can do to help?"

"I wondered if I could ask you a few questions."

"Yeah, okay. But could we go across the hall and do it in my apartment. It just seems strange to be here without...her."

"Sure."

Angela's apartment resembled Stephanie's almost exactly, except she had movie memorabilia hanging on the walls; pictures of film stars from the fifties—Clark Gable, Rock Hudson, Doris Day and a raft of others.

"Interesting photos," I said. "You probably weren't even born when those movies came out."

"My dad loved them. He'd put me on his lap and the two of us would watch. Eventually, I came to love them too. Rock and Clark knew how to make them classy. Not like the movies today. Rock was a man's man."

I wasn't quite sure how to interpret that. So I left it alone.

"I guess that's why Stephanie and I bonded. She did a few movies herself."

I nodded. "Do you have any clue as to who could have killed her?"

She thought a moment. "I'm not exactly sure. But I told the police I saw this man, but they never sent anyone over to talk to me about him."

"Oh? When did this happen?"

"The night of the murder."

"I see. Did he have a ponytail?" I thought it might be Mr. Waterworks.

She shook her head. "No, I don't think so. But he had a beard and walked with a limp."

This was turning into a Humphrey Bogart movie—Sam Spade and the case of the bearded limping man."

"I do remember one more thing. He had a tiny mark on the left side of his neck that looked like a bee."

That cleared a lot up for me. But it got me worried too.

Chapter Twenty-Nine

I couldn't understand why Mickey never got rid of the 'bee' birthmark. At least when he wore the beard and glasses at the restaurant, you couldn't see it.

The birthmark had been one of the first things I noticed when I met him at dental school. He used to make a joke about it. "I may have a bee, but at least I'm not buzzed."

Now you know why he became an orthodontist rather than a comedian.

I needed to talk to him. I drove by his house on Eldridge and saw a "sold" sign on the lawn. He'd moved? So where was he now?

I was about to park and talk to the neighbors when I sensed the car behind following me.

I sped up for a few blocks. It didn't matter. The car stuck to me like it was a sugar-holic and I was a Mars Bar.

The odd part was that usually criminals followed you in big sexy cars. This was a Honda. A Honda from the eighties. I bet this guy had a 'Happy Days' lunch box too.

I turned right, then left, but couldn't lose him. I tried speeding up and taking side streets, but every time I looked out my rear view mirror, I saw him on my tail.

I knew I had to stop sometime so I looked for a place I could drive where there'd be crowds of people hanging out. That way, I'd be protected if this evil mastermind intended to perform any dastardly deeds like trying to sign me up for Amway.

Unfortunately, the only place ahead of me was a used car lot. It wasn't my first choice, but what could I do? I swung the car in a big right turn and headed onto the lot. Out of the corner of my eye, I caught the Honda park across the road next to a Burger Place. I tried to see who was at the wheel, but I couldn't make out the driver.

I jumped out of my vehicle and immediately met something even more frightening than the man across the street—a used car salesman.

He looked rake thin, as if sales hadn't been too brisk of late, and he had a creased face as if it needed a good ironing.

He wore a plaid jacket, a bright red tie and a facial expression that said, "my kids need braces, and my wife's master card is two months overdue." He stared at my car, a 2007 Toyota Camry for a moment and his eyes lit up. "Hi, I'm Dave." He handed me a card.

I looked at the card and saw that his last name was Hastings, and he was the sales manager. At the bottom of the card it said you could phone him 24/7. Great news. Nothing more I wanted to do than talk cars at three in the morning. I put the card in my pocket.

He waited before saying anything else, then I realized he wanted my name. I gave it to him.

"I guess you're looking for something more exciting, Arnie."

I stared at the Honda across the road and said, "uh, yeah, sure."

"Fantastic."

I swear I saw him salivating.

Dave began showing me what appeared to be every car on the lot. I saw Volkswagens, Chevrolets, big cars with air bags, small cars with large trunks, cars with GPS's. I asked questions, pretending to be interested, even though, I hadn't budgeted for a new car till about twelve years after I was dead.

I truly felt bad doing this to Dave. He seemed like a swell fellow. But with the guy across the road watching me, I didn't have much choice.

Dave took me into a tiny office and had me sit down. I knew this was where he would give me the hard sell. The good news for me was that I had a clear view of the other side of the street.

"So what have you decided on, Arnie?"

I shrugged. "Tough decision, Dave. They all look great."

"Well, let me point out the benefits of buying from me. One…"

I didn't hear the rest of the numbers, as the man in the Honda had decided to put me out of my misery and drive away.

I had to get out of here so I came up with a little fib. "You know, Dave, I've been thinking, with Margie still out of work and the kid's wanting to go away this Christmas, I'm not sure this is the right time to buy." Okay, so it was a big fib. What could I do?

He stared for a moment as if I had spoken in Swahili. His face turned pale and he appeared like he might need medical intervention to keep him conscious. I guess he thought we had something special together. I promised myself I'd make it up to Dave somehow.

"Gotta go."

I left the office quickly, deciding not to turn back unless I heard the sound of Dave falling flat onto the cement.

I got back into my car and drove to the restaurant where I had met Mickey as Z.

Chapter Thirty

I don't think much ever changes at the fabulous Three Rings Restaurant, unless every once in a while they rotate the drunks. I sat at the same table as I had before, hoping Sarah would be my waitress. I didn't see her around. A few moments later, a different waitress appeared—blonde hair with red highlights, overdone blush on her cheeks, long fake eyelashes. The natural look.

I ordered a tea. When she brought it, I asked if I could talk to Sarah.

She gave me crossed arms. "Why?"

"Just wanted to ask her something."

"You leave her alone. She's a good kid, never done anything wrong." The anger pulsated through her face and when she fluttered her eyelashes, one of them fell into my tea. She didn't notice. Maybe I wasn't as thirsty as I thought.

"No, no, she's fine. I just needed to ask her something." She glared at me as if I was the guilty one in a police line up. I was ready to say, 'I did it with the crowbar in the professor's study.'

I pushed my cup aside, not thinking green tea and eyelash made a good combination. I usually just put in lemon. A few moments later, Sarah arrived.

"Hi," I said, "Remember me?"

"Uh huh. Tea guy. We don't get many tea guys here." She stuck out her little finger and made a pouring action with her hand as if all us 'tea guys' were very delicate individuals.

"I guess not," I said. "I wondered if you remember the man I sat with the other day."

"Mickey?"

I was surprised she knew who he was, with the disguise and all. "He comes here a lot?"

"Yeah. Always flirts with me. Except when you were here and he wore that getup."

"But you still knew it was him?"

"Oh yeah, sure. He's worn it before. He told me he does a lot of good deeds, and he doesn't want anyone to recognize him. He prefers to give anonymously." She spread her hands. "He's a humble man."

Mickey the giver. Right! At least she did know him. This was good news. I looked up to the heavens to give thanks. In this case, the heavens was a thirty-watt bulb that hung by a thin red wire.

"It's important that I find him. Do you have any idea where he might live?"

She got that far away look in her eyes that people sometimes have when they're thinking really hard about what you asked or trying to pretend they are.

"No, sorry."

"Does he come here at a certain time of the day?"

She shook her head. "No, one day it's for breakfast, another for lunch or supper. The only thing that's consistent is the small tip."

I thanked her anyway, gave her a tip to split with the other server—hopefully bigger than Mickey's.

I'd learned one major fact. Mickey must live pretty close by since he comes here all the time. It didn't help much. Sure, I could come in on different days and see if he showed up, but I didn't have time for that. I levered myself up from my seat and was about to head toward the door, when I felt an arm on my shoulder, and heard a voice—a deep, resonate voice. The kind you might hear on a commercial. However, instead of informing me about the numerous health benefits of Pop Tarts, it said, "Hey, guy, heard you asking Sarah about Mickey."

I looked up to heaven again. Same light bulb.

The man sat down at my table and I joined him. He had straight black hair and seemed as thin as a pencil. I pegged him around sixty, but he looked younger, like he'd had plastic surgery or Botox. When he talked, nothing on his face moved. It was like speaking to one of the presidents on Mt. Rushmore. Though I'm not sure any of them had work done.

"My name's Joe."

"Arnie."

"Cool. Do I look familiar?"

He smiled and showed perfectly aligned white teeth. Actually, they were too white and he probably could get work guiding planes back to airports.

"You've probably seen me before," he said, trying to appear humble. "I'm an actor, did a lot of TV in my time. Kid shows, movies of the week, comedies. I even did a few weeks on a couple of soap operas."

While I enjoyed the theatrical resume, I really didn't know what this had to do with Mickey.

"I might know where your friend is."

"Where?"

"I'll take you to him, but it'll cost. See acting don't pay so good for a man my age. They want these pretty young things. What's with that? I still look good, right?"

"Yeah, sure."

He showed off his teeth again, almost blinding me. "Give me a hundred and I'll show you where this guy, Mickey, lives."

"A hundred? That sounds like a lot."

"Think of it as helping an actor through a rough patch until he gets the Oscar he so richly deserves."

I reached into my wallet and pulled out two fifties.

Chapter Thirty-One

Joe and I walked down several side streets, through a forest, then passed a few alleys. I'm not sure he wasn't going around in circles just so he could tell me more about his illustrious career.

"Then I did a one-man show at the Pasadena Playhouse."

"Very nice, but are we getting close to where—"

"The critics said..." He reached into his pocket and pulled out a tattered, yellowed newspaper clipping from *The Pasadena Times*. He began reading. "Joe Boyle is a refreshing talent, destined to move into the higher echelons of show business."

I checked the date, 1962. Apparently, the only place he went is obscurity. Not that I didn't feel sorry for him.

Most actors' lives were spent trying to become big stars, but tragically ending up like this guy—pulling clippings out of their pockets trying to impress strangers who had other things on their mind.

We finally stopped at a low-rise apartment building. The bricks were cracked and the door had a broken window. I couldn't believe Mickey, an orthodontist, lived here. Maybe it wasn't the same Mickey. Maybe Joe had made a mistake. I didn't know, so for the moment, all I could do was follow him.

He swung the broken door open and we treaded upstairs. We walked through a short hallway with a broken light and stopped in front of room 34B.

Joe knocked and I stood way back, just in case the person behind the door was someone who intended to cut me because he hadn't been happy with the teeth whitening I'd given them.

The door slowly opened and Mickey's downcast face appeared. Yep, same Mickey.

Joe smiled. "Hey, room-ie, sorry, lost my key."

I turned to Joe, not believing this. "You're his roommate?"

"Uh huh," he said, as if it were no big deal.

"You charged me a hundred bucks."

"I took you to him, didn't I?"

I tried to hold myself back from throttling this guy. I'm sure that would have made his face move, Botox or no Botox.

I could see the shock in Mickey's face. "What are you doing here, Arnie?"

I didn't say anything, just walked in and sat down. Beside the couch was a table that looked like it had come from the Salvation Army. On top, lay Mickey's black book. It was open to the 'O's' and I noticed the name Orlando in big letters. He quickly picked it up and stuffed it into his pocket.

"Listen, Mickey, the next time you go somewhere in disguise, I'd recommend a turtleneck."

"What do you mean?"

I pointed to his neck. "The bee thing." Debbie's next door neighbor told me you were at Stephanie's apartment the night of the murder."

The color drained from Mickey's face as if some evil alien creature had sucked out all of his vital juices.

"Yeah, I was there."

He sat down, rubbed his neck hard, as if that would remove the bee birthmark and this whole night wouldn't have happened.

"Arnie, you gotta understand. She was dead when I got there. I had been to her place the night before. We had an argument and she wanted to break up. I left and thought when I phoned her the next day she'd beg me to stay. She didn't and we argued more. I went over to talk to her about it."

"What time did you go?"

"About eight. I knocked, but no answer. So I used my key. When I opened the door and saw her lying on the floor, with all that blood, I felt sick. I truly thought she was my soul mate, Arnie." He looked at me, his face slack, leaden.

I shook my head. "To have a soul mate, don't you actually have to have a soul?"

"Before you get any wild ideas, I panicked, that's all. I'm already in so much trouble, I had to get out of there fast."

"I take it you didn't call the cops?"

"Listen, Arnie, when you're being chased by mob guys who want you dead, you don't wanna have to deal with the police too."

"Well, there's another problem. Debbie's been arrested for the murder."

"What?"

"She went to see Stephanie that night too."

"Why?"

"Why do you think? She thought Stephanie had stolen you away from her."

"Oh, no." He rubbed his head as if he could rub away all his problems." Debbie will get off—right?"

"I don't know. But I think you should come down to the jail and talk to her."

"I don't think I could do—"

"Mickey, she needs you."

"When she finds out I pretended to be dead to get out of marrying her, she'll—"

"She knows. I told her."

His body tightened and his hands started to shake. "She'll kill me. She'll kill me."

Chapter Thirty-Two

I finally convinced Mickey to come with me to see Debbie. He got his roomie, Joe, to disguise him so he looked like a 75-year-old geezer. He would definitely not be listed as *People Magazine*'s sexiest man of the year.

Joe took off, said he had some audition. I drove Mickey to the police station. He didn't want to take his car in case someone recognized it.

I urged Mickey to take off his disguise before he saw Debbie. After all, we were in the police station. No one could get him here, except perhaps the academy of theatrical arts for bad acting.

He agreed.

I decided that it was more important he saw Debbie than me. So I went to Rick's office.

His feet were lying on top of his desk as usual. He looked about the same as last time, only a little more bloated—if that's possible.

"Sorry, Arnie, nothing new on your girlfriend."

"Ex girlfriend."

"Right."

"You still believe she's the Orthodontist Killer?"

"I have a bit more information. We tracked down the orthodontist she had as a child and he said that when he told her she'd have to wear braces, she got pretty upset. That's probably where it started."

I stared at Rick, not believing this. "That's all you got?"

"We also have the fact that since she's been locked up, there haven't been any more murders."

He had me on that one. The lack of murders made it look like Debbie could indeed be the Orthodontist Killer.

I didn't see the point in trying to convince him that he was wrong. I knew it wouldn't do any good. Law enforcement is all cause and effect. If 'A' is in jail for a crime that 'B' did, and the crimes stop while 'A' is off the street, the police believe there is only one solution—'A' did it. Of course, this could have been a devious strategy by 'B.' He was crafty. Don't get me started on 'C.'

Although I would hate to do it, I thought about offering my assistance in the Orthodontist Killer case. However, I knew Rick would refuse, if only because the department would look silly if a dentist/PI solved a crime that the police couldn't.

I went back to the area just outside the jail and found Mickey sitting down. He looked like a guy whose girlfriend just informed him she's going to the prom with his best friend.

"How'd it go?"

"Not well."

"Well, what do you expect? Indirectly, because of all you've done, Debbie's in jail."

"I know. I know. She spent most of the time crying. At least when she didn't yell and make fists. She's got quite the right hook." For emphasis, he made his hand into a fist, then punched the wall. Unfortunately, it was solid cement and his high-pitched scream was probably heard throughout the prison.

"So you're not on good terms right now, I take it."

"No," he said, rubbing his hand. "Do you think I broke something?"

"I don't think so. Don't you care about Debbie at all?"

"Of course. She's a wonderful girl when she's not in jail. Maybe at another time in my life this would have worked out."

He looked at me for confirmation, but I couldn't give it to him.

We got in my car. Halfway back to Mickey's place, he fell asleep. He looked peaceful and I began to think he wasn't such a bad guy after all. Maybe, as he says, it was just the wrong time in his life. Maybe, that was the problem with Debbie and me as well. Maybe, if things had happened at another time, there would have been no obstacles. Of course, that's a lot of maybes and maybe I should have thrown in a perhaps.

I drove on, thinking about all that, when I glanced in my rear-view mirror and realized I was again being followed by the Honda.

Chapter Thirty-Three

I quickly made a sharp right turn and twisted onto a side road, but the Honda kept trailing us. I increased my speed as I yelled, "Wake up, Mickey."

His eyes flew open and he moved his head from side to side, looking all around. "What, what?" He took the sleep out of his eyes and rubbed it onto my freshly cleaned interior. "Geez, Arnie, what'd you wake me for? I was having this beautiful dream about an Island Paradise where these nubile young native girls elected me king and my first ruling was to outlaw underwear. And now it's all gone."

"Forget the underwear."

"Yeah, that's what I told them. You don't need it." His eyes started to close.

"Stay awake, Mickey. Someone's following us."

"What?"

"There's been a Honda behind us for the last ten minutes."

"A Honda?"

"Yes, he's the guy who followed me before."

Mickey looked in the review mirror, then he put his hands on his head. It looked like he might scream or throw up. Or both. Although I doubt he was that good at multi-tasking. "Damn."

I didn't like the sound of that damn. "Would you happen to know who that is?"

He moved his hands every which way that was mathematically possible and a few that probably weren't. We might have to get Stephen Hawking in to explain them.

"Uh, well, there's a small chance I might know him."

"Uh huh."

I waited to hear all about that, but Mickey stopped talking.

"Are you going to tell me or do I have to get out the magic markers and we play Pictionary?"

"Well, it might, possibly, perhaps be one of those guys from Vegas that I owe money to."

I shook my head, not believing what I just heard. I floored it and turned onto Wallace Street.

The Honda did a sharper turn and his car squealed. "I think we should stop and talk to whomever is in that car, Mickey. He is not going to give up."

"They'll kill me."

My foot edged toward the brake to end this nonsense when suddenly, Mickey slammed his foot on the accelerator. We zoomed forward at what seemed like warp speed. I was sure we were going to pass by Captain Kirk in the SS Enterprise.

Suddenly, a huge truck for Alberto's Fettuccini barrelled down the road toward us. It looked like we were going to smash into it and die being part of a side dish.

Mickey screamed, "Look out!"

I turned the steering wheel hard and the car twisted to the right, then jumped up over the sidewalk onto a front yard, hitting a *for sale* sign. My car stopped suddenly and we both almost bumped into the windshield with the second most important part of a man's body—our heads. The impact forced us back onto the seats, gasping for air, but alive.

We didn't speak for a few moments, trying to recover. "That was a close one, eh Arnie?"

I nodded. "Yeah," I said, glaring at the person who caused all this.

He smiled. "I think we're okay, though." Mickey patted his chest and face, then moved his legs back and forth a few times. "Yep, everything's fine and dandy." He patted my arm. "Lucky, I was here with you."

"Right." With all the activity, we had forgotten that there had been someone chasing us. But a moment later, we were reminded of that fact when we heard a car door being shut and heavy footsteps tromping toward us.

I looked in the side mirror and saw that it was the same blonde man who had approached Mickey and me at the restaurant. And this time he had a friend—a 45 calibre pistol. He walked toward my door and grunted the words, "Get out,"

Chapter Thirty-Four

I stepped out of the car, thinking Mickey would follow, but like all rules, he thought he was exempt. He stayed inside, his right leg shaking like it was dancing to Crocodile Rock.

Blondie yelled again. "Get out, Mickey."

Mickey didn't seem to understand. As if for the moment, all his synapses had been replaced by silly putty. Finally, he dropped his hand to his non-partying leg and forced it to move. Little by little, Mickey edged himself out of the car. Blondie, using his metallic companion, directed him to come over beside me.

"Lovely to see you again, Mickey. How you been?"

Mickey gave him a dopey smile, then started rambling. "Good, very good. A little under the weather what with my nasal allergies and digestive disturbances, but not so bad considering."

"Glad to hear it." He pointed toward me. "This the guy?"

"Uh yeah, yeah, that's him."

Blondie got in my face, looked me over from head to toe, like I was a centerfold model. I felt so cheap.

"Didn't I see you before?"

"Yeah, I believe you had the pleasure at The Three Rings Restaurant. Lovely establishment."

"Now I remember. So where is it?"

"What?" I asked, confused.

Mickey jumped into the conversation. "He, uh, didn't bring it."

I looked at both of them. "What are we talking about here?"

"The money, asswipe. You're the money man, right?"

"Uh, well..."

"He is. He is," said Mickey. "Greatest money man there is. I've never met a better money man."

I scowled at Mickey, still very confused.

"Listen, you guys better have the money by tonight or Mr. Peterson will be very upset. You don't want to get Mr. Peterson upset. He's not understanding like me. Who knows what he might do?" Blondie's grin was so wide his ears almost disappeared. I could even see a black tooth in the back of his mouth. Why didn't criminals with all the money they steal, take better care of their teeth?

"Okay, meet me at eight tomorrow night in the alley on Dunkirk. Make sure you have the money." He pushed the gun into my back. "If you don't bring it, I'd think about what cemetery you'd like to be buried in."

Then he got back into his car and drove away.

I stared at Mickey. "What's all this about?"

"Nothing."

"Nothing? The man is going to kill us if we don't deliver money to him."

"I don't think he'd go that far. He's just a little annoyed with me."

"And why the hell would you tell him I'm the money man?"

Mickey smiled a guilty smile. The kind a kid gives when he's pulled a girl's hair and said he didn't do it even though a piece of her hair is still in his hand.

"There's a good reason."

"Yeah? I'd like to hear it."

"He works with those guys I told you about. You know, the ones I owe money to. I made up this story about a money man to get time to come up with the cash. I guess he assumed you were him. Funny how life is, isn't it?"

At this moment, I really didn't think it was all that funny. "He didn't assume. You told him."

"Assumed, told, small difference. So what are we going to do?"

I blew out air. "Don't you mean what are you going to do?"

"Right."

He didn't give me any answer and I couldn't think of anything either. I took Mickey home, neither of us talking all the way there.

When I got back to the office, I saw once again that Tanya had worked her magic. "Why are there thirty patients waiting for me? It was supposed to be a free afternoon."

"Where have you been, Arnie?"

I didn't want to worry her so I told her I had just taken a drive.

"Oh, that's nice, taking a pleasure trip while you have a roomful of patients hell-bent on seeing you."

"Sorry, Tanya, but I got caught up in something pretty rough."

"You don't know from rough. Mrs. Nijinsky said if you didn't come back soon, she was going to start taking hostages."

"I've got an idea. Why don't you send the patients down the hall to Dr. Michaels? Tim told me the other day his practice had been kind of rocky lately. He even had to sell his new Lexis. He'll be happy for the business."

She didn't look any brighter. There wasn't much more I could do. I had things I had to take care of.

I began to walk out when a thought hit me. I pulled the card from my pocket with Dave's Car Dealership information on it and ambled back over to Tanya. "Oh, and give Tim this. Tell him to say, 'Arnie sent him.'" I handed her the card and headed toward the door.

"Where are you going now?"

I mumbled, hoping she wouldn't figure out that I hadn't actually said anything that made sense till I'd left.

I knew if I told her where I planned to go, she'd probably do everything to stop me. But a promise to me is important.

When I got to the jail, Debbie looked sad behind the glass partition separating us. "Everything okay?" I said on the prison phone.

"Yeah, I guess."

Beside me sat an older man who like the guy who had sat there before, looked like a crook. Long unruly hair, snub nose and three days of beard growth. He wore a black leather jacket with a skull on the back and blood coming out of its eyes. I had a hunch he wasn't an insurance salesman.

How come all the guys on the outside look like they should be on the inside? And why did all the people inside look like they should be in Beverly Hills?

"Debbie, I'm trying to get you out, but so far no luck."

"Thanks Arnie," she said, a sarcastic tone in her voice.

"What's wrong?"

"I don't think you should be saying things like "no luck," to someone trapped behind bars eating food that a dog would give a thumbs down to."

I smiled, happy to impart some knowledge to her. "Actually, dogs don't have thumbs."

She grimaced and her eyebrows crunched down. I felt a cold chill fill the room. You'd think by now I'd know when not to share my extensive knowledge of the animal kingdom with a woman.

"What do you want me to say, Debbie?"

"I want you to tell me everything is okey dokey. I'll have you out sooner than you can say saliva sucker."

"Actually, they're not technically called saliva..." Her eyebrows crunched back down. At that moment, I realized I should probably keep my extensive knowledge of dental instruments to myself as well. "Never mind."

I looked at Debbie and thought how hard it must be for someone used to a nice middle-class life, running a flower shop, to suddenly be in jail for a crime she didn't commit. "Do you really want me to lie like that? I thought you wanted honesty."

"I did before any of this happened. But when I realized I wasn't gonna get honesty from Mickey or anyone else, I figured I might as well get lies that make me feel good."

I nodded. "Okay, I'm sure I can get you out faster than you can say...saliva sucker."

I thought I detected the beginnings of a smile on Debbie's face.

Chapter Thirty-Five

That night, I sat on the sofa trying to relax, but my brain raced with thoughts of all that had been happening lately. I decided to watch a documentary on new methods of teeth extraction. Hey, you relax your way. I'll relax mine.

We've certainly come a long way since tying one end of a string to the door, one end to a tooth, and then slamming the door fast. Actually, that used to be my favorite method until the time my door locked and I had to hire a locksmith to get me back into my office.

Speaking of doors, suddenly, I heard a knock on mine. I answered it to find Gino standing in front of me looking menacing. Of course, Gino standing any time, any place, anywhere, looked menacing. Probably, he could sit in a wheel chair with two broken legs and a sprained arm and still scare you.

"Hey, Gino, this isn't about the teeth, is it? My equipment's all at the office. Forks and spoons, electric can openers don't work so well. Believe me, I've tried."

"It's not that. Mr. Rodrico needs you."

I crinkled my forehead. "I thought we solved everything."

It's like he didn't hear what I said. He simply repeated, "Mr. Rodrico needs to see you."

I drew in a deep breath. "Okay, fine, let's go."

During the drive, Gino had his left hand on the wheel and his right hand free so that every once in a while, it could dive into a bag of popcorn that sat beside him.

"Gino, do you really think you should be snacking on popcorn? You know last time you got a kernel stuck in your teeth and it hurt."

"You're right, Arnie. Snacking ain't good." Then he picked up the bag and poured it all into his mouth. His cheeks puffed out like a hot air balloon. He chewed and coughed, coughed and chewed. When he'd finally swallowed everything with several unearthly gulping sounds, he said, "You're right, Arnie, making it into a meal is much better."

Of course, minutes later, he complained about a pain in his tooth. Lucky I always carry my tweezers, and moments later, he was a happy camper. I reached into my pocket and gave him a sucker—sugar free, of course. I told him if he came in for a check up there'd be lots more of those. He immediately said he could make it Tuesday at ten.

We got to the mansion in record time, and soon I was in the study sitting across from my favorite mob boss.

He looked perturbed, but said, "Arnie, I'd like to thank you for helping Phil and me come together."

"Oh, uh, you're—"

"But, unfortunately, I can't."

"What?"

He stood up. "It seems that this has caused more problems than we anticipated."

I didn't like hearing the word *problems* from a mob boss.

"It seems the Darogas are unhappy that two of their own are related to someone in the Larotta Family. And they especially don't like Phil and me coming together like this. I've heard rumors that they're going to do whatever is necessary to prevent the union of the families. And that includes coming after me."

"Can't Phil talk to them?"

He began to pace at a slower rate than usual. This must really be troubling him. "I'm afraid not. He's been arrested."

"What?"

"The police connected him to someone who got whacked. Phil says he had nothing to do with it, but right now he's in the slammer. I have a hunch that someone in the Darogas may have set him up."

Rodrico eased himself up from his chair and gave me steely eyes. "You're the only one who can help us, Arnie."

"I really don't know what I could do."

"You got me to join forces with Phil. I thought that would have been impossible. But you did it. I know you can handle this. You're good at that emotional crap. Me and the boys, we're just gangsters."

I didn't know where to start with this one. So I had Judy connect me with Robert, seeing how he and I had established such a good rapport.

I bet when he saw me he'd give me a big hug. Yeah, that's right. He'd do that, then ask how things were going. And maybe we'd go on a fishing trip together. Ah, who was I kidding? The man was an emotionally-muted gangster who didn't seem to like me too much. He'd probably just as soon shoot my legs off as look at me. Maybe he'd just forget about the looking and do the other thing. But he did say 'yes' to talking. We arranged to meet at a coffee shop on Morris Street.

When I saw the place, I wasn't sure I wanted to walk in without backup. The door had numerous holes which looked like they might have come from a derringer, and I was pretty sure the red stuff smeared on the door wasn't tomato soup. Although, you never know, maybe that was a speciality of the house.

I sat down at a table in the corner and surveyed the other customers who seemed to be watching me with creepy eyes. If I'd hazard a guess, everyone there was a mobster thinking that every other mobster had a contract out on him. I'm sure on travel brochures, this would be listed as an out of the way place where everyone is looking out for you.

Finally, Robert showed up wearing a dark jacket, dark shirt, dark tie. Nice to see him wearing his happy clothes. I often wondered why criminals always dressed in black. At first, I thought they did it to look tough, but maybe it was just so blood stains didn't show up so well.

I didn't get any *hi* from Robert. The first thing that came out of his mouth was, "I told you there'd be problems."

"Yeah, well, maybe we can."

He spread his hands. "This isn't a church group, PI."

"Look, we worked everything out with your dad and Rodrico."

"This is different. Dad's a softie compared to everyone else. Now, Lucky is boss and I think it's gone to his head. A lot of the guys are afraid of him."

"There's got to be a way to fix this."

"There's no way."

I forced my brain to think of something, anything. "I want to talk to Lucky."

The expression that Robert gave me made me think that people who weren't in the mob seldom got a meeting with Lucky.

"Don't think he's gonna wanna talk to you."

"Ask him."

He paused a long moment, before he spoke. "Alright. But it may take a few days."

When he left, I really didn't have high hopes of being able to fix anything. I just didn't want there to be any blood spilled—especially mine. Maybe I should start wearing the black jacket, shirt and tie.

Chapter Thirty-Six

I got back to the office about six fifteen in the evening. As I had hoped, everyone had left. It would give me a chance to think about what was going on with my cases.

I took out my notebook, wrote down Debbie's name, and sketched her behind bars. Then I drew Stephanie dead in her apartment and Mickey leaving. After that, a drawing of Mickey with his new pal, Blondie. In the middle, I sketched myself. On that picture, I wrote, 'money man.' The drawing reminded me of the various scenarios that were in play right now. Of course, my art teacher from the seventh grade probably would have looked at the picture and said something like, 'maybe you'd be happier in the class for the *special* students.

I didn't believe Debbie killed Stephanie, and as much as I wanted to, I didn't think that Mickey murdered her either. Right now, Blondie was the only other suspect, but I didn't know the connection between him and Stephanie. Or even if there was one. That's what I had to find out. I would try to do that tonight when we met with him.

Roommate Joe answered the door at Mickey's place, dressed as a giant beaver. A grey furry costume and buck teeth.

"Nice outfit," I said. "I take it you're not going to be performing Macbeth."

"It's all my agent could get me this week. A kid's birthday party. It's pretty upsetting." He shook his head in frustration, although it's hard to bring off *frustration* when you're dressed as a marsupial.

His buck teeth suddenly banged onto the ground, breaking in the process. He snatched up the pieces, looking sad. "Damn, I'm gonna have to glue them back together again." He walked into the other room, having punctured my illusions about the glamour of show business.

Mickey pranced out a moment later dressed as a large pink bunny—floppy ears, furry body and a fluffy tail. When he noticed me, he seemed embarrassed. I don't know why. Being an orthodontist and dressing up as a giant pink rabbit was certainly nothing to be embarrassed about.

Mickey glared at me. "What?"

"Nothing, except I'm not sure Blondie will appreciate the look."

Mickey's paw started to shake. I knew something was up. "You know, Arn, I thought maybe you could go yourself. When you think about it, you're the one he really wants to see." Big rabbit smile.

Actually, at this moment, he didn't look so much like a rabbit, more like a chicken. I couldn't believe he'd try to get out of it.

"See, with my office destroyed and—"

"*You* destroyed your office."

"Right. Anyway, I have no income right now, Arnie. Joe got me hooked up with his agent and he offered me a gig. I happily took it. It's not much, but it's something." He touched his right ear and it flopped back and forth, like a lazy bobble-head. At least his ears seemed to be secure. Something we hope for in our own lives.

I tried to contain my anger. "Mickey, if you don't come tonight, Blondie is going to track you down and do damage to that pink cotton tail of yours."

"But—"

"Besides, I have a plan."

Mickey took out his wallet and spread it open. Empty. "I need the money, Arn."

"How much are you making tonight?"

"Seventy-five dollars, but—"

I pulled out my wallet and gave him the seventy-five.

He thought a moment, decided something, then picked up the phone and dialed.

"Hello, Abe? Mickey. Listen, I'm a little under the weather tonight and don't think I can do the bunny gig." Mickey coughed several times. Possibly the worst performance given by a rabbit I'd ever seen.

"Uh huh. No, Joe's good to go. Oh, no, I have to throw up again. I don't think the kiddies are gonna want to see that. Yeah, thanks." He hung up. "He went for it. Just give me a minute to change, Arn."

Five minutes later, Mickey came out from the bathroom still wearing the pink bunny outfit. "The zipper's stuck."

Chapter Thirty-Seven

Mickey and I drove to meet Blondie. When we stopped at lights, people looked in and saw a rather normal looking guy, (me, I'm hoping), sitting with a big pink fluffy rabbit. I just hoped nobody I knew saw me. At one point, I sped up a little and a policeman pulled us over. He intended to give us a ticket, but when he saw Mickey, he laughed so hard, he tore it up.

We parked on a side street, beside Dunkirk Avenue. As we walked toward the alley where we were supposed to meet Blondie, I looked at my watch and saw the time—seven-fifty. We had ten minutes of people sauntering by, and giving rabbit-Mickey and me strange looks.

I got concerned when Blondie didn't show by eight-twenty.

"He'll be here," said Mickey. "He's been after me a long time for that money. He's not just gonna give up."

"Maybe he got a load of your get up and decided you weren't being serious."

"Why would he think that?" Mickey said, adjusting his enormous rabbit feet so he wouldn't trip over them.

"I say we give him five more minutes."

"Yeah, sure." Mickey pulled out a cigarette and started smoking.

"Do you really think you should be doing that?"

"Why not?"

"Those costumes are made of flammable material."

"Yeah?" Mickey removed the cigarette from his mouth and tossed it behind him.

"Maybe you shouldn't have done that eith—"

A moment later, I smelled smoke.

"It's your tail," I yelled.

"What?"

"Your tail is on fire."

Mickey didn't understand at first, but then he spun around and saw the flames lighting up his rear end. He kept repeating, "My tail is on fire! My tail is on fire!" Then he started patting his behind and dancing around like a bad contestant on *So You Think You Can Dance*.

He finally managed to put his tail out, but not before a crowd had gathered and wondered what kind of street performer he was.

I wanted everyone out of the area if, and when, Blondie showed up, so I explained the show had ended, and the next one would be in two hours with even more thrills.

People drifted away and a few moments later, *The Blonde One* had arrived. Of course, he wore all black.

He had a puzzled expression as he stared at Mickey. "Interesting wardrobe, Harrison. Although I always pictured you as more of a rodent than a rabbit. I won't even ask why you're wearing it. Just give me my money and we'll go our separate ways."

I stepped toward Blondie. "You don't think we'd just bring it here, do you? We need proof that you won't ask for any more money from Mickey."

"Yeah, sure. I give you my word." He held up his hand, like a boy scout who didn't have any merit badges.

I spread my hands. "A criminal giving his word, that's really reliable. I'm sorry that's not good enough. Perhaps we could trade information. Then I might trust you more."

I could see Mickey's paw trembling again. He moved toward me, spoke out the side of his mouth in a whisper, even though I'm sure Blondie heard every word. "What are you doing, Arn?"

Blondie ignored it as did I. "What kind of information?"

"Know anything about Stephanie Warwick?"

I swear I saw a moment of fear cascade through Blondie's bullet-like eyes. But seconds later, he took out a gun. So maybe I'd been wrong about that fear thing.

At that moment, my idea of Blondie as a people person dissolved into the ether.

Mickey whispered to me out the side of his mouth again. "Okay, now it's time for that great plan of yours."

Chapter Thirty-Eight

I, of course, didn't really have a plan. I've always been more a spur of the moment kind of guy. Works well for book reports, but not so good with angry guys with firearms.

Blondie shook his gun at us. "Okay, I'm through with this talk, assholes. Give me my money."

Suddenly, Mickey came alive. I wasn't sure that was a good thing. "It's at the office. Arnie left it there." He looked at me. "Remember, Arnie. In the bag, on top of the bookcase, beside the *Playboys*, next to the *Newsweeks*." Mickey's imagination amazed me. Also his stupidity. Blondie laughed. A loud wild monkey laugh. Personally, I didn't think he had it in him.

"Alright, so maybe you guys will come with me and make sure I find it."

Mickey stepped back. "You know, now's not a good time for me. I have a lot on my *to do* list."

Blondie pushed his pistol against Mickey's head.

"Yeah," said Mickey, "well, I guess I could do that stuff tomorrow."

We got into the backseat of Blondie's car, but not the Honda—a red Jaguar. He'd been holding out on us. It had a matching red interior and bucket seats. It might have been a fun road trip, but that gun sitting in the front seat kind of put a damper on things.

Neither Mickey nor Blondie spoke during the drive. I guess they didn't want to disturb the delicate sounds of nature wafting in through the windows—birds, bees, trees swaying in the wind. I didn't speak either, but in my case, I just didn't want to be a dead money man.

When we arrived at my dental office, Blondie parked, grabbed his weapon and we all went upstairs. Old friends. And, thank goodness, up until this point, alive friends.

We sauntered down the hall to my office, the lights still on. Blondie seemed puzzled. "I thought this place would be closed by now,"

I checked my watch. Seven-thirty. I was surprised too. I usually closed the office by six. What was going on?

"Doesn't matter." He put the pistol in his pocket and whispered that we better watch what we said. Then he had us walk in. He followed.

Tanya greeted me in a more upbeat mood than I'd seen from her in a long time.

"Hey, Arn, how are you doing?"

"Good, great."

My mouth formed a smile that probably looked as frozen as the tofu turkey I get at Thanksgiving.

"I told Dr. Michaels he could close his office and work on the rest of the patients here. It was wearing him down going back and forth. That okay?"

"Yeah, sure, fine." At that moment, I noticed Tanya wore a silky blue gown with matching high-heels.

"Why are you dressed up?"

"Date tonight with Milton."

"Who's Milton?"

"You know, the guy I've been seeing."

"Mr. Hair Weave?"

She nodded, a g-force smile on her lips. A moment later, however, Tanya noticed Mickey and her lips instantly reverberated to free-fall. I knew there was going to be trouble.

Chapter Thirty-Nine

Tanya glared at Mickey. "What the hell are you doing here? I've got a few choice words to say to..."

I broke in. "Uh, Tanya, Mickey's here to, uh, help on a case. See my cousin, Roger..." I pointed to Blondie. "...he, uh, needs some big dental work."

She looked at Mickey like he was meat past its prime. "I can't believe you're using him after what he did to Deb..."

"Yeah, well, the thing is, he's still the best orthodontist in town. So I gotta work with him, right? Anyway, we should get going. Roger is in a lot of pain. See you in a while."

I moved away fast and led Mickey and Blondie to my office. After we entered, Blondie slammed the door. He looked around trying to find the money. I had a hunch he might not find it since there wasn't any. He turned to Mickey, upset. "I thought you said it would be on the top of the bookcase. This guy don't even have a bookcase. Whatcha trying to pull, Harrison?"

"Well, uh..." Mickey scratched his head as if he were totally baffled by this. Like it was a greater mystery than Stonehenge. Then he glared at me, and started yelling. "Where the hell did you put the bookcase, Arnie?"

I couldn't believe he was blaming me. Thinking fast, I said, "I, uh, had to move it out. It didn't seem appropriate somehow, in a dental office where I see patients."

He came back with, "I had a bookcase in my orthodontist office."

"You did? Why? You're doing dental work. You don't have the space for things that—"

"It made things more homey and—"

"But it detracts from the professional—"

Blondie's face got *angry*-red. "Forget the damn bookcase, numbskulls; where the hell is the money?"

I pointed to the filing cabinet that had a few magazines on top. "In there."

Blondie marched over, tugged at the drawer, but it wouldn't do his bidding. "Give me the damn key."

I pulled a key off my key-ring and threw it to him. Mickey gave me big eyes behind Blondie's back and started making weird hand signals that indicated he intended to attempt some risky manoeuvre that would save us both or that his blood sugar was low and he was going to lapse into a hypoglycaemic coma. At this point, I sort of thought the coma thing might have been preferable.

Blondie opened the cabinet, took out my carefully color-coded patient files. When he didn't find money, he came at me with both hands raised in claw-like formation—like a lobster with arthritis. Not his most attractive pose and I'd suggest he not use it as his profile picture on any dating websites.

As he came closer, his rage seemed to increase exponentially. I had to do something so I grabbed the first thing I could think of—my drill. I began drilling into Blondie's neck.

He screamed for a moment, then slammed me into the wall and clutched my throat tight. He removed the gun from his pocket and pushed the hard metal into my chest. "Drop it."

I dropped the drill.

"You try anything like that again and you're a dead man!"

In the corner of my eye, I noticed Mickey watching as if he was in a movie theatre enjoying the show. The only thing he was missing was a box of Milk Duds.

A moment later, Blondie's face relaxed as if he'd just had Shiatsu Therapy. He even said, "Nice office," just before he turned into a one-man demolition crew. He snapped a bunch of toothbrushes I give clients into many bite-size pieces, threw my tray of dental instruments onto the floor and stepped on them. Then he twisted my drill into some kind of origami shape. I think it may have been the *Flapping Bird*.

"I can keep going like this, or you can tell me where the money is."

I hoped Mickey might say something that would be of great help to us, that would change everything and get us out of this desperate situation. But after he saw what Blondie had done, he seemed to have quieted down for some strange reason.

Things were at a standstill. In front of me stood two unstable figures—one, a criminal with a gun, and two, an orthodontist with a runaway brain. I had a hunch the more unstable personality was number two.

I hated to think it was going to end like this.

Suddenly, there was hope—a knock at the door. I knew it was Tanya. I looked at Blondie. "I've gotta get that or my receptionist will think there's something funny going on."

He pointed the gun at me. "Go, but be cool."

"The thing is she's very suspicious about everything. She's gonna think it's odd if you're up and about. You're supposed to be getting treatment. You better sit in the chair."

He shrugged. "Okay, fine, but nothing funny." He walked over to the chair and eased into it.

As he did, I moved toward the back of the chair where the gas controls were and turned them on full blast.

His head snapped around toward me. "You did something, didn't you?"

"No, I—" There was another knock at the door.

He looked toward the door and I pushed the gas hose onto Blondie's face. I grabbed the gun from his hand, threw it to Mickey. He came out of his coma and caught it.

Blondie struggled to get the mask off while I struggled to keep it on. I could feel his strength hard against me. I kept pushing. He finally got it off and forced it onto my face. I began getting sleepy. I could hear Tanya outside, yelling my name. I was too tired to say anything. With one final burst of energy, I pulled the mask off my face, pushed it onto Blondie's. I was still groggy, but somehow found the strength to keep it there. A moment later, he fell into a deep sleep. I told Mickey to hold the gun on him as I answered the door.

Tanya grimaced. "It took you long enough."

"Yeah, I had a bit of a problem with Roger."

She looked inside and her brow wrinkled. "Is Mickey holding a gun on him?"

I nodded. "The gas was causing a bit of a reaction and we had to get tough."

"Come on, Arnie, what really happened here?"

Mickey smiled smugly. "Don't worry about it, Tanya. I took care of everything, no problem."

Chapter Forty

We called the police and Blondie went to jail. Because of that I didn't have to see Mickey again. Also good news.

After that incident, I had a special button installed in the arm of my dental chair. When I pushed the button, Tanya would hear a buzzing sound at her desk, indicating I was either in desperate trouble or wanted to order the 'Two for One Hot Wing Special from Buffalo Bob's.' It might come in handy in the future. Good discounts like that are hard to come by.

This morning, it was back to work at the dental factory. But first, I told Dr. Michaels I wanted to speak to him about something and asked him to come into my office. He ambled in, smiling. Of course, he always smiled. His lips seemingly couldn't form any other expression.

I asked him to have a seat in my dental chair and I began my little speech. "Listen, Tim, I'm sorry for making you do so much of the heavy lifting in my office lately. I know you still have some of your own patients. It's just that I've been doing, uh, some other things lately and I needed backup."

"Actually, I wanted to thank you, Arnie, for letting me work on your patients. Yeah, I have a few people I still see, but not many. I need the work, got to keep my dental skills sharp. Besides, I enjoyed it. You have some great clients."

"I know."

"And thanks for giving me Dave's card. He fixed me up with a Mustang. Great car, and very reasonable. He asked when you're coming in to get yours."

I didn't know what to tell him about that, so luckily at that moment, my cell phone rang. I apologized to Tim and took the call. "Hello?...hey Robert...oh...you know, now's not exactly a good time. You see—"

"If it's not now, it won't be. Lucky's not the easiest guy to pin down. And if you don't come today, that's it."

I could feel my shoulders tightening and all Mrs. Yama's hard work dissolving like Alka Seltzer in water. "Sure, sure, be there in an hour."

I hung up and smiled at Tim. He gave me his usual smile back, obviously not realizing what I had to tell him.

"Listen, Tim, uh, I have to go out and..."

"Love to help, Arn."

I'm sure my face showed shock. I thought he'd just been nice when he said all those things about enjoying the extra work. Obviously, Tim loved dentistry as much as I did.

"I owe you one," I said. "Lots more than one. Maybe a few hundred."

He left, his feet seeming to not touch the ground. Tanya entered, handed me a yellow file. "Mr. Lawrence is next, Arnie."

"Actually, Tim is going to take care of the patients."

"Again?"

"I have to go somewhere."

"Where?"

"Uh, I have a meeting with one of my clients and—"

"You are not going to leave me in a room with fifty angry patients, Arnie."

I shook my head. "They won't be angry, they'll have Tim."

"He's not you. They want you! You're supposed to be their dentist."

"I'll be back soon; just tell them I had an emergency."

"Oh, there'll be an emergency alright, as soon as they find out you're not here."

Chapter Forty-One

The address Robert gave me was for a small storefront with the name Fortune Investments. I walked in and didn't see anyone. There were desks but no one sitting at them. It was like it was deserted. A moment later, Robert appeared. "You're late."

"Sorry, I got here as soon as I could. I had to do battle with an angry receptionist."

"What?"

"Nothing."

"I'm gonna have to pat you down."

He began patting. Everything went fine until he came to one of my trouser pockets.

"What's that?"

"My Periodontal Scaler."

I pulled it out and his eyebrows raised. "That could hurt someone."

"It has to be sharp to get the plaque off."

"This is a meeting not a dental appointment. You have to leave it with me."

"Right." I handed it to him. "Don't do any dental surgery while I'm gone."

He didn't seem to get the joke. I have a feeling he didn't get too many jokes.

"Walk down the hall. Lucky's in the last room on the right."

I was a little concerned that perhaps something else might be waiting for me in the room. I headed down the hall, all my muscles tensing with each step. I pressed the acupuncture points on my wrist that Mrs. Yama had taught me, but today, they seemed to tense me up even more.

I came to the door on the right and opened it. A man sat at a desk reading the *L.A. Times*. The paper covered most of his face. On the back page, I noticed an ad for beer.

"Mr. Chimera?" I said, feeling funny speaking to a bottle of Heineken.

Nothing happened for a moment, then slowly the paper moved aside and Lucky's stern face appeared. He had a receding hairline and a large chin. Most people show a little vulnerability in their face; he had none. I was surprised to see that he wore a white shirt. Maybe he was one of the good guys and didn't break anyone's legs, just bent them so they couldn't salsa anymore. He placed the paper on the edge of the desk, smoothing out the corners. Meticulous.

He gave me what I thought to be a nod of recognition, but I didn't know for sure. It could have been a secret signal to someone hiding in the closet to whack me.

"Mr. Katz."

"Yes." I put my hand out to shake, but his hand didn't come out to greet it. Just like Robert. What was it with these mob guys? Maybe they were saving their strength for stranglings. I imagine when you had to do three a day, it really must take a toll. My hand drifted to my side.

"Have a seat."

I sat on the wooden chair in front of his desk.

Lucky drew in a breath of air as if he could tell by smell if I was someone to be worried about. He didn't register anything, so I guess I smelled pretty good.

"I'm only seeing you because of Robert. What's this about?"

My arms and legs had locked, but somehow words tumbled out of my mouth. I prayed they were the right ones. "I'm acting on behalf of Lou Rodrico."

A weird expression filled his face. Kind of a cross between having a bad piece of salami and realizing you've killed the wrong man. I'm guessing a guy like him would feel worse about the salami thing.

"I see. I'm afraid then, the meeting is over."

"I'd just like to discuss—"

"I know what this is about, Mr. Katz. But the north side and the south side have always been separate— with their own methods and organization. To combine them would be a big change. I don't like change. Do you understand?"

"Sometimes change can be good."

He considered that for a moment, then his now tomato-red face indicated that in this case, it wasn't.

"Look," I said. "All that's really different now is Robert has a sister. It shouldn't affect mob business."

He gradually levered himself up from his chair. Just when I thought that was all of him, there turned out to be more. If he didn't stop soon, his head was going to break through the ceiling.

"Mr. Katz, Rodrico and I were once friends. Then he double-crossed me and since then we've been on opposite sides. I've made it clear to Robert that he can either stop seeing his sister and stay here with us, or leave. It's up to him. He has until today to decide.

Chapter Forty-Two

The next day, I heard some good news and some bad news. The bad news involved another orthodontist death—Allen Rudolph. I'd heard of him, very popular. The murder occurred in the same way as the others—arch wire wrapped around his neck.

The good news involved Debbie. Since she'd been locked up at the time the murder occurred, she couldn't possibly be the Orthodontist Killer.

Yet, she was still a jail-bird. I decided I had to talk to Rick about letting her go. And I knew the only way to get through to him was to give him the dinner he bugged me about. Sometimes, a little food can bribe someone better than money. I made sure I took an extra 97 cents for Rick's dessert.

It turned out, however, that he wanted something with a little more class this time. So instead of Taco Bell, we ate at Cheerleaders, a steak house in the east end of Corral.

The place, about an hour's drive away, reminded me of a warehouse—lots of space, with brightly-lit yellow walls. I immediately felt a happy vibe surround me. It might have been the hubbub of ordinary conversation and laughter, or perhaps the waitresses dressed in skimpy cheerleader outfits.

In between staring at our menu and our waitress, Lisa, Rick ordered steak. I got salad. We talked about his cases, his last relationship, and did I think that Lisa gave him extra onions as a signal that she wanted him.

I told him I wasn't sure onions were the secret language women used to communicate, but, hey, what do I know.

Yes, a lot of subjects came up, except one—Debbie. I was about to mention her when Rick stopped force-feeding himself his steak for a minute and eye-balled me. "You must really want something bad to bring me here."

"I do. Look, you now know that Debbie isn't the Orthodontist Killer, right?"

"Probably not," he said, seeming to inhale the sweet smell of fat emanating from the gristle on his Porterhouse.

"She can't be. Another orthodontist got killed while she sat behind bars."

Rick tapped his fork on his plate. It looked like he was attempting to get his meat to jump onto it. "She could have had one of her men do it."

"You've met Debbie. There's no way she has men. She had to hire someone to help her organize her shoe closet."

"Okay, maybe you're right. Perhaps she had nothing to do with the murders."

"So why don't you release her?"

He paused a moment, seeming disappointed that the meat was still sitting on his plate and he'd actually have to pick it up with his fork. "I don't know. Is dessert on the menu?"

"Yes it's on the menu."

"Okay; she's out," he chuckled. "Actually, I'd planned to do it anyhow." He shifted in his chair. "But you better keep your eye on her."

I promised Rick I would. Although, I had a hunch with Debbie, that might be a hard promise to keep.

"Now to important matters—dessert."

After the meal, Rick went back to his office and I went to see Debbie. I sat behind the glass partition and told her the good news. Of course, she was thrilled. We chatted a bit, then the guard came by, and opened her cell door. She hugged me big-time outside the jail.

On the car ride home, she asked a ton of questions—like someone who had just been awakened from a cryogenic chamber after a hundred years.

"Thanks for getting me out, Arnie."

"You're welcome. But look, you're not out of hot water yet. I promised Rick I wouldn't let you leave town."

She thought about that one a moment. "Is Orange County out of town?"

"You're not going to Orange County or anywhere else."

"No?"

"No."

We didn't talk about anything substantial the rest of the way. When we got to her place, I walked her to her door, then said goodbye.

"Come in."

"I don't think so, Debbie."

"Just five minutes."

Maybe it was a good idea. She'd been away from the outside world for a while and needed to get used to it again. I entered her large spacious apartment with the pillows on the floor and the yellow couch that I always told her was too lumpy. We chatted for a few minutes.

"I feel so great being back home. It's like I get another chance at life."

I grinned. "Debbie, you weren't a double murderer. You were just mistakenly identified as a criminal."

"I know. But it feels like I can start fresh."

"That's a good way to look at it."

She rubbed my hand. "Listen, Arnie, I know I got angry at you a few times, but it was so frustrating being in jail."

"Don't worry about it."

"I want you to know that I really appreciate what you did." She stared into my eyes and kissed me softly on my lips. A second later, she pulled away, a grin appearing on her face. "Do you remember what happened the last night we saw one another?"

"Yeah, you got arrested."

"Not that part. Us. We were talking about getting back together."

"Oh, right." So much had happened since that night.

"I had a long time to think about that. You know, maybe it is a good idea. Jail made me realize how much I've missed you."

She moved forward, her arm stretching out like she was about to hug me or throw one of those right hooks Mickey had mentioned. I moved away, just in case it was the right hook. "Debbie, you know I would love that. I'm just not sure now is the right time for us to be thinking that way."

"Why not?"

I put on my playful expression. "You are an ex-con. I don't know if a man in my position can associate with someone like that."

I waited a few seconds, but the joke didn't land like I hoped it would. "Look, until we find out who murdered Stephanie and, for that matter, all the other orthodontists, we can't think about that stuff. We have to show beyond a shadow of a doubt that you are innocent of everything. Besides, right now, my mind is on that speech I have to give tomorrow at the Dental Association, and I can't have anything distract me."

"You'll ace it. You're great at stuff like that."

I spread my hands. "The problem is I only have the first paragraph and Tanya wasn't impressed."

She held my face in her hands and slid her lips in slow-motion against mine. We kissed for a few moments and I felt like I was in another world. It was as if everything I ever wanted was here, right now. Our lips were chummy for a few more minutes, then Debbie lifted her mouth from mine. That grin was back again. "You're right, we should wait."

It was too late for me now and she knew it. Something had clicked inside the reptilian part of my brain and I pulled her down onto the sofa and kissed every part of her.

Chapter Forty-Three

I left Debbie's place about twelve, knowing I had to work on my speech in the morning. When I got home, I tried to get a little sleep, but couldn't. I finally put on my cd *Whale Music*. The melodious sounds of these enormous majestic undersea animals never failed to relax me, mostly because I knew the whales were way down in the ocean, not in my living room.

The next morning, I had a small breakfast and got right to work. Unfortunately, the first lines I wrote involved global warming and how it's affecting the enamel on our teeth. What that had to do with accepting an award for being dentist of the year, I wasn't sure. But after writing for a few hours, I finally finished what I thought was a pretty good speech.

Tanya called to check up on me and when I told her I'd finished, she wanted to hear it.

"Look, you're gonna be there tonight. It'll be a nice surprise."

She didn't seem to agree about the nice-ness of the surprise, but said, okay.

"So, what are you wearing, Arnie?"

"I thought I'd put on my checked sports jacket and my stripped blue shirt. You know how good I look in–"

"No, you're not."

"What?"

"You're not wearing that."

"Yeah, I am."

"It's a special occasion, Arnie. We need to go shopping."

"That's not necessary, Tanya."

"I'll be there in ten minutes to pick you up."

"Tanya..." But it was too late. She had hung up and was probably on the 409 freeway, having already received two of the three speeding tickets she was sure to get.

A short time later, we were at Rolley's Department Store trying on suits. Well, I tried on suits. Tanya busied herself with telling the salespeople that what they were wearing was all wrong. She was a master at getting rapport.

The first five try-ons went by in a flash. When it came to my sixth suit, Tanya decided that I had a winter complexion. "You know, like skiers." Which was strange, since I didn't ski, didn't like skiing and didn't even like people who skied. In fact, the only winter sport I participated in was the 'snow shovelling and freezing your butt off event.' I believe the judges would have awarded me an 8.9.

Tanya handed me several jackets that were almost glow-in-the dark.

"I don't think I need anything this bright, Tany. Cars aren't going to come at me while I'm giving my speech to the dentists."

"You look best in intense, rich colors, like navy blue and pastels.

The salesman disagreed, took away those jackets and gave me several light gray ones.

Tanya grabbed them from my hands and replaced them with *winter* jackets. Then she moved toward the salesman like she was going to do something very painful to a certain part of his anatomy.

Suddenly, he smiled at me and said, "My mistake, of course, you're a winter, you should be wearing more intense, rich colors."

I guess the poor guy realized he wouldn't be able to sell her anything if he didn't agree, and calming Tanya down might allow him to have children in the future.

After trying on what I imagined were a hundred and seventy-two more jackets, I finally made a decision, which actually meant, Tanya had finally made a decision.

The suit was light blue with subtle gray pin-stripes. The wine-colored tie she'd chosen had very tiny dots that I worried would hypnotise my audience into sleep. Hey, I didn't need any extra help to do that.

When I finally stepped in front of the fitting room mirror, I had to agree that I looked great. Maybe even dapper, like someone who would be dentist of the year.

"You look beautiful, boss." Tears began rolling down her cheeks.

I didn't know she'd have tears in her eyes later too, but for a very different reason.

Chapter Forty-Four

That evening, Tanya and I drove to the Ellsworth Hotel, located downtown near City Hall. It had been around since the sixties. Movie stars, sports figures, famous rock'n'rollers had all stayed there.

We walked arm and arm into the elegant hotel lobby. Every part of it radiated class. There were swirling red patterns on the fluffy carpeting and ornate gold-framed pictures of celebrities on the wall. I have to say, I did feel like a bit of a celebrity myself.

Tanya wore an elegant black evening gown, backless I might add, which accounted for the male population of the room seeming to be all behind her. A string of jade pearls hung around her neck and her wrists had matching jade bracelets. Plus, she showed cleavage that could convince a monk to give up his vow of silence and say, "wow."

The most seductive item in her arsenal was the happy look on her face. She took hold of my hand. "Listen, Arn, I just wanted to say, I'm very proud to work alongside you."

"I'm proud to have you aboard, Tanya."

We ambled down the hall to the ballroom, about to enter, when I heard a familiar voice yell, "Hey, Arnie."

I turned around and saw Leo Simpson, a dentist I had gone to school with. He had come from a wealthy background but was a regular guy. He hadn't changed much, still had that twinkle in his large green eyes and that midnight-black head of hair. As always, he dressed very stylishly. Armani, I think.

"Congratulations, my friend." He shook my hand.

"Hey, Leo, thanks."

"Arnie, you really deserve this. I'm glad they finally recognized you."

What a wonderful man. I remember during dental school days, he lent me money when I struggled with tuition. His large eyes suddenly got even larger, like an actress when she finds out the man at the bar is a movie producer. "And who's this lovely lady?"

"It's my receptionist, Tanya. You've never met her?"

"No. I would have remembered someone who made my heart beat fast and my eyes roll around in my head."

Tanya's face contorted into an expression I'd never seen before. "The heart's okay, but I think you should have that eye thing looked into."

Leo giggled.

Tanya grabbed my hand. "We should find our seats."

"Just before you go, Tanya," Leo said. "If you ever want to assist a real dentist, give me a call." He handed her his card.

"Don't do it, Tanya," I said, winking at her. "He'll make you do that thing you don't like—you know, work."

Another giggle from Leo.

As we said our goodbyes and walked away, Tanya whispered to me, "Was all that just a sales pitch to get me to be his receptionist?"

"I don't think so. I think he likes you, but he felt uncomfortable asking you out with me here."

"Oh."

"You've already got Mr. Hair Weave anyways, right?"

"Yeah, Yeah," she said, watching Leo as he sauntered away.

We entered the ballroom and told the man at the desk our names. He handed me a card with our table number on it.

The tables in the ballroom were spread around the outer edges. In the middle of the room, there was a big floor space for dancing. I didn't think that would be used much tonight. Dentists are not known for their tango.

I noticed a lot of security. I guess that had to do with the recent killings in Corral. Good idea. Although I doubted it would help much. I knew from experience that if a murderer has plans, he'll find a way to do it. Still, I was glad that the organizers were at least taking precautions.

Tanya and I found our table, number twelve. It looked onto a platform where various board members of the Corral Dental Association sat at their tables.

Tanya and I took our seats and looked around the crowded room.

"Are you nervous, Arnie?"

"A little. But hopefully once I get on stage, I'll be okay."

A moment later, the rest of our table appeared— Doctors Tate, Mann, and Reynolds. Tate brought his wife as did Mann. Reynolds came alone. Two of them I knew fairly well, however, Mann was an orthodontist and, of course, I had no contact with him whatsoever.

The dentists were all talking shop. Mann kept to himself. That's generally the way it is. Dentists are social butterflies, while orthodontists tend to be loners.

The platform resembled the one at the church where Debbie was supposed to have been married. It started me thinking. Not a good thing.

I guess Tanya could sense my downward spiralling mood. "You stop that, Arnie Katz. Tonight is your night. You shouldn't be thinking about anyone else but yourself. And maybe what kind of expensive gift you're going to get me for being your escort."

"You're right. I have to just focus on enjoying the evening."

As the night wore on, it got easier to do that. The food tasted wonderful—filet mignon, lush green avocado salad with cherries and strawberries topped off with walnuts. Not to forget, pistachio ice cream with a sweet and sour mango sauce that made your tongue quiver with excitement. I had to un-quiver that little guy. He had a speech to give tonight!

After a wonderful dinner, the lights on the stage brightened. Dr. Sears, the head of the Dental Association, appeared—the light reflecting off his shiny bald head. He picked up the microphone and began speaking in a low gravelly voice.

"Welcome everyone and thanks for coming. Today we're here to honor one of our own—Dr. Arnold Katz. In the years since he's begun his illustrious career, Dr. Katz has contributed a tremendous amount to the dental field and the community. He has set up programs for seniors where they can come to his clinic for free dental work. And he has an outreach program for the homeless. Each year, there is his annual charity picnic for underprivileged kids and he often gives talks at the schools about dental care. Of course, as many of you know, that's just the tip of the iceberg. So let's all welcome to the stage, this year's selection for dentist of the year—Dr. Arnold Katz."

The crowd exploded into applause. Now, I felt my stomach quiver. Great. I had a quivering stomach and a quivering tongue. If anything else quivered, I'd be doomed.

I walked up the three steps to the platform. Dr. Sears handed me the mike and whispered, "Congratulations."

By time the applause stopped, I felt better. "Hello, everyone. I want to thank you so much for this award. Of course, I'm a dentist, so the first thing I thought was how could I melt this down and use it as a filling." Big laughs!

"I think the important thing with our association is not what we do as dental practitioners. Sure, we should better the lives of our patients and improve their oral health. But sometimes, we have to step outside the dental community and make contributions to society as a whole."

The crowd erupted into big applause with people standing and applauding. I guess I hit a chord with them.

I had planned to do some jokes about my practice, then weave in some touching material about my mom who always told me it didn't matter what I did as long as I enjoyed it.

But I didn't get to that part because a loud explosive sound reverberated in the ballroom.

Chapter Forty-Five

Someone else might have thought the air-conditioner had exploded or a waiter had dropped a whole pile of dinner plates. But, as a PI, I've heard that sound many times before—a gunshot. I felt okay, saw no blood on my white shirt so I assumed I didn't get hit. Then I looked behind me at the platform. I saw Edward Larson, an orthodontist, and ex-professor of mine, covering his chest with his hand.

I bounded over to him. Edward was still breathing, but his face looked green. I wished I could have just yelled out, "Is there a doctor in the house?" But, of course, we were all dentists.

I got Tanya to call for an ambulance and then I glanced around the room searching for anyone who didn't belong. No one looked out of place.

A moment later, however, I saw a flash of black and white running out of the ballroom.

I jumped off the stage and followed the flash. I ran out the door as fast as my brogues could carry me, then sped down the hall. I saw the person running and could now tell it was a man. He wore a suit and tie like everyone else in that room so he had obviously pretended to be in the dental field to get inside.

I gained on him, but then a waiter moving a food cart got between us. I dashed around the cart, lost the runner for a minute, then saw him race up the stairs. I cobbled up two stairs at a time, breathing heavily. When I got to the top, I looked in both directions, but didn't see anyone running.

I took a moment to let my breath lapse into more normal breathing patterns, then headed back to the ballroom, upset that I hadn't caught him. I entered the ballroom and saw Tanya standing on the now-deserted platform where Edward had been.

"What happened?" she asked.

I shook my head, still gasping for air. "He got away. How is Edward?"

"They took him to Swansea Hospital."

"Did you hear anything?"

"No."

I told Tanya I needed to go to the hospital and gave her money for a cab to go home. She handed it back, said she wanted to go with me.

We drove, not saying anything for a while. I guess we were both still in shock. Then at a stoplight, she started peppering me with questions.

"Did you know Edward well?"

"He taught some of my courses at dental school. A lot of the professors didn't seem to care about their students. But he did. I remember I told him I had doubts about whether I should be a dentist. That I didn't think I had what it took. He told me that before he went into the field, he had doubts about himself too. But he's never looked back on that decision. He said that he thought it would be a good fit for me too—that I had what it took. That's probably the reason I became a dentist."

We parked at the hospital and rushed inside. I found out Edward was on the fifth floor in intensive care. We took the elevator up and I asked the nurses about Edward's status. They said they'd tell us when they knew something.

We sat on the most uncomfortable chairs in the world and drank bad coffee while we waited. Tanya and I tried to talk about other things, but the conversation kept drifting back to Edward. Finally, a doctor came out and said he would be okay. The bullet hadn't hit any vital organs.

Tanya and I hugged one another. The doctor told us we could talk to Edward, but Tanya said, I should go in myself.

As soon as I walked into his room, I could see Edward had the old spunk back. He wore his professor glasses like the old days, at the bottom of his nose. Although he was in his seventies, he didn't have a wrinkle on his face.

"Hey, Arnold. Bang up speech tonight."

I chuckled. He always liked to make jokes. I guess that's why we got along so well.

I sat down on a chair beside the bed. "How do you feel?"

"Okay for a guy who's just been shot."

"The doctors say you'll be out in a few days."

"I don't know if I want to go. The food here is better than the stuff Marjorie makes me at home."

"Where is she, by the way?"

"She couldn't come tonight; she's been under the weather herself. She just called. I assured her, I'm fine, but she insisted on coming now. I hope she's not bringing any of that food." He chuckled again, then he gestured toward me.

"Thanks for helping, Arnie."

"I didn't do anything."

He pursed his lips. "I think you did lots."

"Did you see anything? What the guy looked like?"

He shook his head. "Not really. I'm sorta thinking it might be that Orthodontist Killer fellah."

I nodded. "Possible. But what's odd is that there were lots of orthodontists here tonight. But you were the only one who got shot."

"Yeah. And the thing is I'm a bit different than the other guys. I've been teaching at the College for years; haven't treated a patient in a long while. So it couldn't be someone whose bite I made worse, right?"

"Perhaps this guy is older and you treated him when you were in practice."

"Maybe," Edward said, sitting up. "Owww, that hurts."

"You should get some rest. The police will probably want to talk to you."

"Yeah, I'm looking forward to that." He rolled his eyes. I like to think I taught him the eye roll.

I said goodbye and that I'd be back to see him again. Then I walked into the waiting room. I told Tanya he was in good spirits and that seemed to make her happy. Just then my cell phone rang. "Hello? Hey, Deb...How are you...What? Cameras? Are you sure?"

I couldn't believe what she told me!

Chapter Forty-Six

I stormed into Rick's office. "What the hell you doing videotaping Debbie?"

He took his feet off his desk and sat up. "How did I know you were going to...you know, do some wild stuff with her?"

"You have that on tape?"

"The officers made a mistake and put one of the cameras in the bedroom. We caught some things we probably shouldn't have. But no need to worry, you looked great. Did some moves I've never seen before."

I calmed down a bit and glared at him. "Were you hoping Debbie would say something you could use in court?"

"Look, this is a murder investigation; I have to keep my eyes on things, so to speak."

I gave him a look that could have melted steel. "Well, keep your eyes off that."

"Okay, I'll take the cameras out."

At that moment, it became clear that I couldn't depend on anyone else's help. I would have to find out who killed Stephanie by myself. Otherwise, Debbie would always be under a cloud of suspicion. I put my hands on Rick's desk and leaned toward him. "I'd like to talk to that blond guy in prison."

His expression didn't change even when he told me the bad news. "He's dead."

I stared at him as if he had just told me that King Kong had invaded the city. "How?"

"It happened last night. We don't know how. The ME is examining the body right now."

This really put a damper on my plans. I had hoped Blondie would be able to give me some information about Stephanie's death. But now that trail was no more.

At least Rick had told me where the cameras were located. I left his office and phoned Debbie, told her to cover them up with newspapers until the police arrived.

"Why don't you come over, Arnie?"

I paused a moment to think, to make sure I said the right thing. "The other night may have been a mistake, Debbie. You're still under investigation and we shouldn't be doing things like that right now. Maybe never."

Chapter Forty-Seven

Later that day, I decided to visit someone who might be able to help me in solving Stephanie's murder—Benny "Squeaky" Gordon. He's an ambulance-chasing lawyer.

Usually when you think of lawyers, you imagine guys dressed in Armani suits practicing law in corporate glass towers. Benny wore jeans and an old cardigan and worked out of what used to be a dance studio. I'm surprised he didn't come out wearing a leotard, performing Swan Lake. Who doesn't want a limber lawyer?

You're next question is, of course, why is someone who has a law degree working as a snitch. Well, after he'd been arrested for lying under oath, stealing a car and shoplifting a few choice items from Lucy's Lingerie, (He claimed he only wore them on the weekends) they sent him to prison. Oddly enough, a lot of people are not fond of hiring a jail-bird lawyer. So he lost a lot of clients. He blamed that on me since I was instrumental in putting him away.

I sat down in his waiting room with no magazines, no pictures on the walls, no windows, hoping he'd come out soon.

I first heard a little giggling, then I saw him as he sauntered out with a young blonde wearing a short leather skirt. Her lipstick seemed to be smudged. She adjusted her blouse and it appeared as if Benny was about to spank her. I'm not sure that's proper legal procedure after a meeting, but Benny's the lawyer so I guess he would know. Then he noticed me and instead, reached for her hand and shook it. Professional.

Benny looked about the same. Round body, round face, round ears. He was bald on top, but had heavy thick sideburns that consisted of more hair than any rock musician had on their head. He wore a green jacket, purple jeans and a yellow plaid shirt. I take it he got dressed blindfolded today. The girl left and he ambled over to me.

"What do you want, Katz?"

"I need a favor."

"A favor? After what you did to me?"

I smiled my most charming smile that I only bring out two times a year. Once at Christmas, and once when I'm trying to get Tanya to be reasonable during salary negotiations. "It's important."

"What do I get out of it?"

"The satisfaction of helping a friend."

He grimaced, bit his lip, then said, "ow," then bit his lip again. Not the most co-ordinated fellow.

"I don't think so."

"How about the fact that, said friend, is not interested in any recent offenses that you may have committed."

"What offenses? I'm as clean as a self-flushing toilet."

"Oh, so you're not doing the gambling thing anymore."

He gulped, all the color leaving his face. "Why don't we talk in the office?"

I followed him into his office.

Stacks of rumpled file folders sat on his desk, the corners bent out of shape. Legal books were stacked beside them, I guess, to make it look like he knew something about the law. Actually, I guess he did, only it was how not get caught breaking into places and what to do if you are.

But I was hip to his tricks. I knew underneath his desk, he had a computer set up so that he could place bets on races all over the world.

I sat down on a chair that looked like it belonged more on a sundeck than an office. He took a seat on the same kind of chair, and pursed his lips. "So what is it, Katz?"

I leaned my arms on his desk. "The Warwick murder. Do you know anything about it?"

He didn't flinch, didn't move one nasal hair for a moment. Then he shrugged. "Sorry, can't help you." He stood up as if the meeting had ended. I stayed seated.

"You sure you never heard anything about it?" I asked.

"If I did, I'd tell you, you know that."

I nodded, then picked up one of his file folders and looked through it, found a racing form from the Woodbine Track in Canada and one from a track in Jamaica. He really got around.

"That's fine," I said. "But I'll be talking to the cops in the next few days and I just hope I don't accidentally blurt out anything about your illegal betting operation. You know, I kinda have loose lips about things like that."

"Maybe I do remember something."

He sat down.

"Okay, look, I'm not sure, but I think the Warwick woman had been seeing Orlando Peterson."

Stephanie had another guy on the line? She was one busy woman. "That name rings a bell. Who is he?"

"He and his goons are into everything from horse racing to prostitution."

"What's he look like?"

"A little hefty, short. Maybe two to three hundred pounds."

My brain tossed me a thought—maybe that's the guy Daniel Richards told me about. He said Stephanie had been hanging around a fat man. "Do you think he had anything to do with her murder?"

He shrugged and his eyes began darting around the room.

"What do you know, Benny?"

"I can't tell you anything else. If he finds out, I'm a dead man."

I held up the racing form again. He adjusted his body as if his shorts were too tight. "All I know is that she had something of value. There's a rumor he killed her or had something to do with it. But it's just a rumor."

I looked at his face and realized he probably didn't know anything more.

I asked him where Peterson might be but Benny had no clue about that either. Looking at his jacket again, I realized that he didn't have a clue about much.

I left his office and ambled to my car muttering the name, Orlando Peterson, to myself.

Where did I know that name from?

Chapter Forty-Eight

I knew I had to check out the name. But I had something else on today's menu first. I needed to see Rodrico to get the scoop about the trouble between him and Lucky.

I sat at the desk in his study, right across from him. He was wearing a black jacket and tie, of course. He seemed troubled. I didn't like seeing him that way. Of course, it would depend who the trouble was with. The Family? The entire United States, or me? He poured himself a scotch and Lisa brought me a green tea. At first he didn't want to reveal anything about him and Lucky. But after a few moments of thinking, then pacing, then more thinking, then more pacing, he spilled.

"I knew Lucky when I went to college."

"You went to college?"

He nodded. "Yeah, right here in Corral. Took some accounting courses. You know, just in case the crime thing didn't work out." He pushed a book on his desk to the side.

"Anyway, Lucky and I became buddies, at least, I thought so. Then one day, I met a girl. We weren't in love, but we were friends. What I didn't know was that Lucky loved her. When he found out about her and me, he thought I'd double-crossed him and blew his stack. I tried to explain that we were just friends, but he never believed me. That's the last conversation we had. It's what led to him and Phil starting their own organization."

"So this girl broke you two up."

His eyes seemed sad. "Yeah."

"Maybe she can bring you back together."

"What do you mean?" He furrowed his brow.

"Where is she now?"

"I don't know."

"Do you remember her name?"

"Lucinda."

"Her last name?"

He shrugged. "It doesn't matter. Lucky is never going to change his mind about me."

"The last name?"

He inhaled sharply. "Jones."

I left the office, not feeling hopeful. The girl's name couldn't be an unusual one like Chompsky, Michelbrow, Dingleweedler. Something that would be easy to find. No, it had to be Jones.

I spent the next several days in between dental appointments phoning every L. Jones I could find. I hit 102. Lucy, Laura, Linda. Not to forget, Larry. But no Lucinda. Who knew if she was even still single or hadn't moved?

Finally on a Saturday afternoon, I hit the jackpot.

"Hello?" the sultry voice said.

"Lucinda?"

"Yes."

"I wondered if you happened to go out with a Lucky Chimera back in the seventies?"

A pause. "Yes."

"Would it be alright if I met you at a coffee shop and we talked?"

"Who is this?"

"I'm a private investigator and it would help me a great deal."

Another pause. "I guess."

Half an hour later, I met Lucinda at Peter's Donuts and Dry Cleaning off Winton Avenue. I always thought it was wrong to combine those two businesses together. When people left, they wouldn't be able to fit into the clothes they just had cleaned.

I found Lucinda in a corner booth drinking a coffee and munching on a cruller. Beside her plate was a cleaning ticket. I decided not to tell her my thoughts on this place.

She told me she'd be all in red. And she was—red blouse, red skirt, red shoes. It emphasized her shimmering blonde hair and electric blue eyes.

"Lucinda?" I said.

"Yes."

"Arnie Katz." I sat down at her booth.

"So what do you wanna know?" she said, sipping her coffee.

"Anything you can tell me about Lucky."

Her eyes looked up to the ceiling trying to force her mind to access old thoughts, feelings. "I loved him. I knew he loved me too, but for some reason he kept stalling about marriage. Maybe he had commitment issues, I don't know. I realized I had to move on. Soon after that, I met Lou Rodrico. He and I got along great, but we were more like friends. Lou knew that too. There's a little voice inside your head that tells you when it's right and when it's wrong."

"Are you married right now?" I asked.

She shook her head. "Divorced. Why, you interested?" She giggled, a beautiful sound.

"I'm, uh, sort of involved right now," I said, not knowing my actual status at the moment, and wondering if I would ever know. "Could I talk you into seeing Lucky again?"

Her eyes opened wide. "That's a long time ago."

"What's that little voice in your head saying now?"

"I don't think so. It's too long..."

"Listen, all I want is for you to talk to him. It could help a lot of people if you did."

"I don't think so."

Chapter Forty-Nine

I stared at Lucinda wondering why she would say no.

"It's just that Lucky and I didn't end on good terms, and I don't think he'd be happy to see me."

"Lucinda, all of Corral, California, could be in trouble. You could save it."

Her eyes opened wide and I could see her mind working all this out. But she was a rock and I couldn't figure out whether she had. In a little voice, I heard, "Okay."

"Thank you."

I told Lucinda I'd pick her up tomorrow and take her to Lucky's house. Today, however, I had to rush back to the clinic for my four o'clock appointment with Roberta O'Leary. She was one person who wouldn't let Dr. Michaels work on her. It had to be me.

I 'hi'-ed Tanya and hurried into my office. Moments later, Miss O'Leary, a sweet grey-haired woman in her seventies snuggled up into my dental chair. If anyone met her, they would think she was very normal, almost shy. And they'd be right. But when I'd give her the gas, she'd suddenly morph into a wild and crazy lady. I don't mean she'd act strange. She'd act STRANGE! She would actually change into another personality.

On one occasion, Florence Nightingale made an appearance. On another, Cleopatra came by for a visit. One time it was Freud and she/he tried to psychoanalyze me. Kept on telling me that I had a sexual problem and that's why I went into dentistry.

She was so convincing, I even looked at the shapes of my dental instruments and wondered if she had a point.

Of course, I always tried to talk her out of the gas, but she insisted that she have it. Even when she just came in for a cleaning!

As I looked at the sweet lady sitting there, I thought I would have liked to lock her in with seat belts. Unfortunately, it was a dental chair, not a Volvo. "How are you doing, Miss O'Leary?"

"Fine, Arnie. How about you?"

"Could be better. Have too many things on my plate right now."

"Maybe you should get a bigger plate." She laughed, then felt her cheek. "Oww."

"Hurts bad, eh?"

"Yeah."

I examined her mouth and realized that she had an infected root. I would have to perform an extraction. I broke it to Mrs. O'Leary as gently as I could. It didn't seem to bother her. Of course, I knew why.

"So you're gonna give me the gas?"

I smiled. "I thought maybe we could try freezing today."

"I don't like freezing. My cheek feels like a rock after that. I want the gas."

I nodded, concerned about how that would go. I decided to set the dial at a lower level than usual. I placed the nozzle on her nose and had her inhale. I hoped she would fall asleep.

Nothing happened.

"Where's the gas, Arn?"

I couldn't fool her subconscious. All those characters in her mind wanted to get out. I had no choice. I covered her nose with the nozzle again, and turned up the dial. A moment later, she fell asleep. Maybe it would be different this time.

Just in case it wasn't, I reached for my extractor and pulled the tooth out as quickly as I could. I removed the nozzle and waited for her to recover so I could send Miss O'Leary on her way.

Suddenly, her placid face morphed into anger and she jumped out of the chair.

"You okay?"

She began unbuttoning her blouse. "What is thou-est doing? Trying to stop me from riding through the streets unfurrowed on my trusty stead, Heraldo?"

I looked at her, puzzled for a moment, then it hit me. "Lady Godiva?"

"Yes, that is I. I am here to protest the taxes. They are too high. They must be lowered so the common folk can afford them. There is only one way to protest this unfairness." She undid another button.

"You can't do that here, Miss. O'Leary."

"I see-eth. You are one of them. Stay-est back." She picked up my saliva evacuator and aimed it like a gun. "Stay-est back now."

No one had ever used my evacuator as a weapon on me before. I knew I needed help. I pushed the secret button under the arm of my dental chair. Three seconds later, my saviour appeared—Tanya. She stood ready to tackle this mighty foe—a 73-year-old gray-haired lady.

"Are you a friend or one of the king's men in disguise?" asked Miss O'Leary.

Tanya pointed toward herself. "Friend. And you are?"

"Lady Godiva, of course."

"Oh. Well, I'm with you on the tax thing, honey. Let's work together. Maybe we can also figure out how to get some pay raises for receptionists."

I could see Miss O'Leary starting to come around. Tanya did her buttons up, then took her into the hallway. As they left, I heard her sleepily ask Tanya where she would find her steed, Heraldo.

I sighed with relief when she left. Well, at least, I had removed her tooth before things got totally out of control. Last time it had been much worse when she was Misty O'Shea who worked at The Naked Lounge and wanted to give me a lap dance.

Before my next patient, I had a little time to make a call. "Hello, Mickey?"

"What do you want, Arnie?"

"You don't have any rabbit gigs tonight, do you?"

"No, it's kinda slow."

"Good. I need to talk to you about something."

"What?"

"I remember a piece of paper I saw on your fridge. It had a name on it—Orlando Peterson. I'd like to come and ask you some questions about him."

He hung up.

Chapter Fifty

Judging from the reaction so far from both Mickey and Benny, this Orlando guy must be one tough cookie. I just hoped I could get more information out of Mickey about him.

I drove over to Mickey's place and dashed up the stairs. My doctor said I should get more exercise. I think he'll be impressed. I'll tell him all about it when I'm in the hospital having my new legs put in.

I knocked on Mickey's door and he answered, only opening the door a few inches. "What do you want?"

I forced the door open causing him to fall flat on his back.

"Hey, what's going on Mickey? I thought we were buddies. We've had so many fun times together."

He stood up. "Listen, Arn, I'm actually going out. Should have left an hour ago."

He forced me back toward the door. "See you later."

"Look, I know this Orlando guy has you worried."

"Shh...don't even say his name."

"You're in your own apartment. We're alone. He can't get you here."

"I'm not so sure about that. He has people everywhere." He looked suspiciously at his closet.

"Tell me about him."

His shoulders raised toward his head. Usually that indicated someone is nervous or doing a bad impersonation of Frankenstein. "I can't."

"Why not?"

He walked back and forth for a few moments like a tiger in the zoo, angry his meat was late. Then he sauntered over to the couch, sat down and almost curled up into the fetal position. I took the chair beside him. "What's the problem, Mickey?"

He lifted his head. "People die around Orlando."

"What do you mean?"

I could see the tension in his lips. "Stephanie's dead and so is Blondie. And they're not the only ones."

"How'd you know about Blondie?"

"I have my sources."

"What's the connection between Blondie and Orlando?"

"Blondie worked for Orlando. That's why I'm so nervous. I'm thinking he had something to do with the murder."

"Why would he?"

"I don't know. Maybe it's because he was worried some information would get out or perhaps he didn't like the idea that Blondie screwed up. Who knows?"

"Were Stephanie and Orlando together?"

He paused a moment, old hurts flashing across his face. "She told me she'd broken it off with him. That was enough for me at the time. No one had died yet."

So Orlando must have been the fat guy that Dan Richards complained about.

"Who else died?"

"What?"

"You said someone else died too."

I could see Mickey starting to sweat. A lot.

He didn't say anything, just took a handkerchief out of his pocket and began wiping his face. The sweat kept coming. Then he inhaled deeply, and walked into another room.

I didn't know where he went or if he'd come back. But a moment later, he re-appeared with a small black wooden box. He held it delicately between his hands.

He opened the box almost in slow motion, showed me the contents.

I'd never seen anything like it before.

Chapter Fifty-One

The box held a white bone-like object, probably made of ivory. A piece of gold had been welded onto it. The bone glistened like it had been polished by twelve maids working around the clock. I mean when they weren't a-milking. I could see my reflection in the gold. Mickey placed the object on the table, handling it like it was 5000 years old.

"Orlando dives for buried treasure. Well, he has people dive for him. With his weight, he'd probably sink right to the bottom. When Armando, one of his divers, first showed him this, Orlando knew he'd found something important. The diver had no clue about it and sold it to him for fifty bucks—a very small sum for a prize of this magnitude."

I leaned closer to Mickey, something I don't like to do too often. But he hooked me with his story.

Mickey moved his hands excitedly in front of himself, attempting to indicate the importance of his words. It looked like he was doing sign language for Koko the Gorilla.

"Orlando took it to Stephanie."

"Why?"

"Because of Daniel Richards. He was a small time antiquities dealer. Orlando figured she could get information from him about its worth, where to take it, etc. Daniel had the object dated for her and discovered that it had been crafted in the Neolithic Period."

That explained why Stephanie started asking Daniel so many questions. Maybe he'd been looking for the bone at Stephanie's apartment. It surprised me what a hamster can get involved in. I nodded at Mickey. "Interesting."

Mickey's hands fell to his sides. "You're not getting it, Arnie. No wonder I became an orthodontist and you're just a—"

"What's the bottom line?"

"Previously, scientists believed that Homo sapiens, who lived in the Neolithic Period, were only producing objects made out of wood." He picked up the bone from the table. "But this proves they also worked in ivory and gold. That's a major discovery, making this one of the most exciting finds of this century. It's probably worth a million bucks."

"A million?"

His eyes lit up. "Possibly more."

I gasped. I didn't gasp often, trying to cut back.

Mickey continued. "Orlando figured there must be more objects like this on the ocean floor. So he tracked down Armando again and asked him to explain exactly where he found it. He said, "in *the Round.*"

"*The Round*?"

Mickey nodded. "It turns out there's a section in the Pacific known as *the Round* because of the way the waves swirl. You know, like in a hot tub."

I nodded.

"Orlando hired divers to see what other treasures they could find. He located other interesting artefacts. But none as valuable as this." Mickey picked up the bone from the table and placed it back into the black box.

"Stephanie had a bunch of artifacts in her apartment. But none of them were anywhere near as valuable. Still, they were worth something. I guess that's why someone stole the artifact from her shelf."

"Why would she keep something even a little valuable on her shelf?"

"That was her philosophy. She felt that if she put it there, people wouldn't think it was worth anything."

"Which one was stolen?"

"The bracelet with the tiny figures."

"It was black?"

He nodded his head enthusiastically, causing his whole body to nod. He looked like a marionette with issues.

"When did this happen?"

"The night of the murder."

"How do you know?"

"I saw Stephanie the evening before and the bracelet was still there."

I take it you didn't tell anyone that either."

"I couldn't." He turned his hands palm upward as if to say, "I'm not hiding anything," or show off that his hands were clean. Still, I got the impression there were things he wasn't telling me.

"Armando must have figured out that the bone had value and attempted to steal it back from Orlando. They caught him and a few days later, he was dead."

"How do you know all that?"

"Blondie mentioned it to me because he wanted to make sure I knew what could happen to me if I didn't repay my loan."

"So what happened with the artifact?"

"Stephanie found someone in a Swedish Museum interested in making a deal. However, before Stephanie could complete it, she was killed."

"How did you end up with the bone?"

Mickey shrugged. "That's not important."

"C'mon Mickey, level with me. I can't help you otherwise."

His lips contorted into a shape that could appear in a Salvador Dali painting. "I found it when I went to see Stephanie the night of the murder."

"You knew she had it, didn't you?"

"Yeah. One day I saw her putting the box in her desk drawer, then locking it with a key. I asked her about it, but she wouldn't tell me anything. But gradually I got her to open up about it."

Mickey tapped the box. "Arn, I'm in a desperate situation right now with Orlando. So when I saw Stephanie dead, sure I felt horrible, but taking the bone gave me a way I could fix things. I knew where she kept the key to the drawer. I opened it and took the box. I had plans to contact Orlando and say someone sold it to me. That I would give it to him if he released me from the gambling debts."

"I guess mentioning that you were the one who actually took it in the first place, might not be a wise idea."

"Right. I was going to, but then I changed my mind because of all the deaths."

"Does Orlando know you have it?"

"No. If he did, you'd have to contact me in the great beyond. Right now, I believe he's desperately searching for it. I'm not sure I should even return it." He held it up against his shirt. "Don't you think it makes me look cool?"

I glared at him. "I don't think hanging out with Jay-Z would make you look cool."

He got an *oh, really* look on his face and plopped down onto the couch.

I put an *uh huh* expression on my face and plopped down on the couch beside him, hoping the synchronicity of our two great minds could help us solve this. I guess I forgot that one of those minds belonged to Mickey.

A moment later, we both got spooked when the door creaked opened.

Chapter Fifty-Two

Both of us calmed down when we saw that it was only Mickey's room-mate, Joe, dressed as a vampire.

"Hey, guys, I vant to bite your neck."

Mickey giggled. "You crack me up every time with that line. How'd it go at the party?"

"Not good! The guy was sixty-five years old and told me I was a terrible vampire—called me Count Hack-ula."

Mickey stared at Joe. "Unbelievable. You're a born vampire, Joe. What do these plebeians know?"

"Thanks, Mick." Joe pointed to the bone in Mickey's hand. "What you got there?"

"Oh, uh, just some, uh, costume jewellery."

Joe tried to take a closer look at the bone-thing. Mickey quickly dropped it into his pocket.

"Didn't know you had stuff like that or I would have asked to borrow it sometime, you know, when I impersonate Madonna." Joe swivelled his hips and sung a few bars of *Like a Virgin* and I wondered who the hell would pay for that.

"Anyhow, I'm off to get changed. I've got another party in an hour. Gotta dress up as a horny gorilla for a retirement party."

He went to his room, leaving Mickey and me back at square one trying to figure out what to do. Mickey withdrew the bone from his pocket and rubbed it as if it was a cherished family heirloom. I actually thought of it as *the bone of death* since several deaths were associated with it. Still, it did look beautiful.

I asked Mickey what he planned to do now. But he continued staring at the bone, almost going into a trance. Knowing Mickey as I did, I shouldn't have been surprised that he would be attracted by shiny things.

Despite Mickey's free fall into never never land, I had made a decision. "Mickey, Mickey—"

His eyes un-tranced. "What?"

"I need to talk to Orlando."

That worried expression appeared on his face again. "Orlando? Why?"

"If we don't find out who murdered Stephanie, Debbie will probably spend the rest of her life in jail."

"But she's out of jail."

"Yeah, for right now. However, she's still the only suspect. And if no others appear, she could go back."

It seemed like all his energy had suddenly disappeared. "I didn't realize..."

"Do you know where he is?"

"No. No idea whatsoever. Sorry. Wish I could help."

I stared at him. "You're lying, aren't you?"

He blew out air. "Alright, I do know." He raised his right hand in an open palm. A body language gesture that indicated he was now telling the truth. "But don't you realize the pressure I'm under here, Arn. The man's a killer and I've got this...this...thing here that belongs to him. Plus, I owe him money. Do you expect me to just take you to him?"

"It would be nice."

"I can't."

"Mickey, you have to return the bone."

Mickey's face turned Kabuki Dancer-white. I could tell that he didn't want to give it back. And I'm not sure it had anything to do with any fears about murders, etc. I think he just liked it. Shiny things.

I knew it had to be done. Debbie's freedom was at stake. And if Mickey didn't care, I certainly did. "Okay, so where is he?"

"You don't want to see him. Did I mention he doesn't use deodorant? Got to stay at least five feet away."

"Listen, this is the only way to clear Debbie's name once and for all. She deserves that."

His shoulders dropped, his face sagged. He looked like a punch-drunk fighter. "Yeah, you're right. Okay. So what do we do?"

"We tell Orlando we'll find out who took the bone."

"But we already have it."

"I know. We'll use it as a bargaining tool. It'll help us get you out of your gambling debts, and get info from him about who killed these people. Hopefully, that will help Debbie."

"Sounds good. Let me know when you're done."

"The first step is for you to tell me where Orlando is."

"He lives in the country."

"Take me there."

Mickey started breathing heavy.

Chapter Fifty-Three

Mickey finally agreed to show me Orlando's location. Joe needed a lift to his birthday gig, so fifteen minutes later, the three of us were on the road—The Rat Pack—except instead of Frank Sinatra, Dean Martin and Sammy Davis, we had Mickey, me and a horny gorilla.

A car zoomed up beside us and Joe decided to stick his head out the sun roof and flip people off, evidently thinking that no one could get him for it. I guess in his primate brain, he didn't realize our license plate was on full view.

The car beside us sped away quickly, probably calling a zoo, telling them their gorilla was loose and that he seemed to have learned the finer points of our language. We let Joe off at a house in the Cherry Hill area, leaving Mickey and me alone. Not my favorite situation.

Neither of us spoke as we drove back onto the main road. I put on the radio to some country station and heard some guy singing about losing his girl and his dog and how he missed Sparky. Apparently that was the girl's name. I was really getting into the song when Mickey chose to speak. "Do you think we can really make this work, Arnie?"

"We have to try. For Debbie."

I could feel his eyes on me.

"I guess I treated her pretty badly."

"Pretending to be dead to get out of marrying her is not your finest moment."

"Yeah, I know." He tightened up his seat belt. "Arnie, did you ever love anyone? I mean really love them."

I didn't have to think. "Yeah, once."

I glanced at him, saw a sadness in his face that I'd never seen before.

"I don't think I ever have. I mean at first, I loved Debbie, at least I thought I did, but then it faded. A short time later, I met Stephanie and thought I loved her too. But then as the wedding date came nearer, I began to have doubts. I'm not sure I've ever really loved anybody. You know, I never thought I'd say this to a dentist, but I envy you."

I smiled, not believing what I just heard. I never thought Mickey had one feeling bone in his body, but maybe I'd been wrong.

He adjusted his seatbelt again. "You think there's something wrong with me?"

"Maybe you haven't met Miss Right yet."

He knitted that thought into his mind like it was part of a cardigan. "Maybe not."

We kept quiet for the rest of the trip, both of us probably thinking about what we did wrong in our lives. I'm sure Mickey had a lot more to think about than me.

We had driven for about three hours and the scenery hadn't changed too much—one block had big trees, small trees, brown grass, the next block showed off small trees, big trees, green grass. I mean I love nature as much as the next person but I'd probably seen enough flora and fauna for the rest of my life. "Where the heck is this place, Mickey, Saturn?"

"Patience, Arnie. Patience. We should be there any minute."

"That's what you told me an hour ago."

"I've only been here once so it'll take me a while to figure out my bearings. But so far, I'm sure we haven't hit it."

I was ready to hit something and Mickey was the closest object. Luckily, after a few more minutes, he pointed to a dense forest area. Great, more trees. Lots of them. But in behind, a large white warehouse rose up, totally out of place—like a chicken standing in the order line at a KFC.

As we got closer, I stared in disbelief at the size of the warehouse. It occupied the space of a football field or eighteen Shaq's placed end to end. "What does Orlando do there?"

"That's where he refines the stuff he finds in the ocean."

I pursed my lips and nodded. A talent I acquired at a young age and hope to pass on to future generations. I drove the car up to a wire gate and got out.

We both stared at the gate. It covered the entire area in front of the warehouse, and about seven Shaqs laid end to end. A sign on the front of it read, "Private Property, Keep Out!"

"You know, Arn, maybe we should forget the whole thing. He doesn't look real keen on company." Mickey turned around and started to walk away.

"How are you at climbing?"

He spun back to face me. "Climbing? You kidding me? If the Lord had wanted us to go that high, he would have given us longer legs."

"I'm going up," I said. Mickey's eyebrows crinkled as I grabbed the gate. Each of my hands held on tight as I climbed up. Every time I looked down, I imagined a pool of Piranhas lay below me and one was giving me the eye. So I knew I wouldn't fall.

At first, things went smoothly, but then about half-way to the top, my shoes began sliding out of the small wire holes. I held tighter onto the fence and using all my strength, forced myself further up the gate.

I was exhausted and my hands felt like they were going to fall off—which would have made it extremely difficult to give quality dental care. I closed my eyes and pulled myself up with all the energy I had left. When my hands rubbed up against the top of the fence, I felt spent, but strangely alive.

I jumped down to the other side of the fence, and now stared at a doubtful Mickey through the many small holes of the fence. It looked like Mickey was in some kind of cage. Somehow that seemed right.

"Come on over, Mickey."

"I don't think I can do that, Arn."

"This is your chance to redeem yourself in Debbie's eyes."

He thought a moment, then moved closer to the fence.

Mickey grabbed hold of it, but couldn't get his enormous clown feet into the holes. I tried to hold his shoes in place, but they were smooth on the bottom and kept slipping out. I could see it just wouldn't work.

We tried for a few moments more, but then Mickey jumped down and said, "That's it, I'm done. Besides, I don't want to drop this." He reached into his pocket and pulled out the black box with the bone inside.

I was in shock. "You brought it with?"

"I couldn't leave it at home. Who knows what could happen to it there."

"You mean in the vault you have underneath your floor. No, it certainly wouldn't be safe. That's the first place crooks would look."

"How did you know where I kept it?"

"I'm a PI, remember?" I moved close to the fence. "Put it away."

Mickey dropped it back into his pocket.

It was a bad thing that Mickey had the bone with him. And I was worried that sometimes bad things attract other bad things. And that proved to be true.

"Halt!" said the military-like voice. It sounded like someone who could take on Hulk Hogan, The Rock and maybe even Richard Simmons when he was exercising to the Golden Oldies. I turned around to see who the voice belonged to. He was tall, muscular with a steel-smooth face and cropped brown hair. His open white shirt revealed a bounty of chest hair—always good for a bad guy. I mean, if you can't even grow hair on your chest, how bad can you be?

He strode over to Mickey, pointed a gun in his back. I walked a few feet toward him to try and help when I heard heavy footsteps behind me and then felt a gun in my back.

Mickey's guy pulled out a key, clicked it into a box on the gate. The gate slid open and the two men took us over to the warehouse, and maybe to our doom.

Chapter Fifty-Four

We entered the warehouse. Inside, it resembled a meat processing plant like I had worked at as a student. Except for the fact that there was no meat. On various tables were objects similar to the ones I'd seen at Stephanie's. Men in white coats would feed them into machines and they would exit cleaner.

Mickey and I were taken to a dark corner and tied up. The guy who had escorted me in had disappeared while Mickey's man sat on a chair in front of us, holding a gun.

I missed my guy.

Mickey whispered, "I knew we shouldn't have come here. I told you."

I didn't want to admit it, but he might have been right. Maybe there was a better way than this to find out what we needed to know.

It was too late now.

A moment later, my guy joined us. I felt a little misty-eyed seeing him again. I got a better look at him this time and figured out why his steps were so heavy. He was chunky and his shoes indicated he had feet that may well have been the size of watermelons. Good luck on impressing the ladies, Big Foot. He wore jeans and a T-shirt and had a throaty voice that seemed to come from way down in his body.

"Hello, my friend, Mickey, and great to meet you too, Mr. Katz. I am Orlando."

He seemed pleasant for a bad guy, but I really don't think tying up people is the way to build a social network.

He spread his lips, showing off a gold tooth in the middle of his smile. Mickey stared at it as if he were trying to catch his reflection.

"I'm curious why you guys were trying to break into my warehouse."

Mickey opened his mouth, but nothing came out except, "uh, well, we, uh..." I could feel his body shaking.

Seeing as how Mickey, the master communicator, didn't seem to be getting too far, I decided to take over the reins. "I believe we can help you."

Orlando's bushy eyebrows rose and looked like they were going to take up permanent residence on the upper part of his forehead. "That's a nice change. Usually people want to borrow money." He laughed at his own joke.

"I heard you were missing a certain...object. We'd be willing to find it for you."

"What object would that be?"

"The bone with the piece of gold attached to it."

A quizzical expression filled his pudgy face. "I won't even ask how you knew about that. But say you were to perform this service for me, what would you want in return?"

"Mickey doesn't owe you anything and you give us some information."

Suddenly, Mickey found some words, but maybe not the best ones. "And fifty grand."

I stared at Mickey to see if his brain had been replaced by an alien life form. Then I looked at Orlando, afraid he might find some of his own words and tell chair-guy to "fire, shoot, kill."

But the only thing that happened involved Orlando's eyes. They suddenly moved down and to the right. According to what I knew about body language, that meant he was actually considering what I'd just told him.

"What is the information you're seeking?"

"Who killed Stephanie Warwick?"

I saw a rainbow of emotions pass through Orlando's face—from hurt, to fear, to anger. I suppose the mention of Stephanie's name is what caused it. "And why would you want this information?"

"My friend Debbie is under suspicion for Stephanie's murder. She's out of jail right now. However, if the police don't find the perpetrator, she'll probably go back and spend the rest of her life behind bars for a crime I know she didn't commit."

He rubbed his hand over his overly pock-marked face, then tromped over to the man in the corner who had been watching us. "Andre, escort them upstairs."

Andre nodded, not saying a word.

We were untied, then taken over to an elevator. Andre pushed the third button down and we had lift off. A few moments later, we entered a fancy dining hall. There were several tables, each with linen tablecloths and crystal drinking glasses. Andre had us sit down at one of the tables in the corner. A few moments later, Orlando showed up and took a seat at our table.

They were very hospitable for evil masterminds. We enjoyed *Chicken a La Orlando* and champagne. Then for desert, Black Forest cake. It almost seemed as if we were at a four-star restaurant with friends, but I changed my mind about that when I saw Andre sitting in the corner with his derringer aimed at us. Personally, I think the man needed a hobby.

Chapter Fifty-Five

The dinner with Orlando made me feel increasingly anxious because I didn't know what was going to happen next. Like last Christmas with the relatives. My Uncle Phil, a war veteran, threatened to pull the pin on his cheese ball and blow me to smithereens. Apparently he didn't like the socks and underwear I gave him.

When we finished eating, Orlando sat back in his chair, pulled out a Montecristo cigar and began puffing. "Hope you enjoyed your meal, gentlemen."

Mickey nodded, more relaxed now. "Yes, but the chicken seemed a tad dry."

I looked at Mickey, unable to fathom the depths of his stupidity. And I was sure they went way deep. We were sitting with a man who had probably killed more than a few people and he's telling him he's no Galloping Gourmet.

Orlando didn't say anything, so I piped up. "But very tasty. I like dry."

He chuckled. "You guys are like a bad comedy team." He broke out into a laughing fit, but then he had trouble catching his breath. He removed a pill from his pocket and swallowed it. "Heart medication. I'm in a stress-filled business so sometimes the old ticker has to work overtime."

He nodded toward Andre who then put the gun away and left.

"Let me start from the beginning. For several years, I have been looking for the lost city of *Goren*. It existed in the Neolithic Period. The people were farmers as well as artists. They created artifacts out of glass, gold and bone. For example..." Orlando pointed to a wall where a small model of a human figure had been mounted. It looked to be made entirely of glass.

"Somehow, the inhabitants were able to carve it simply using handmade tools. Experts I've shown it to say they are completely puzzled as to how they did it. Even today, with our technological advances, it would be very difficult to create these objects."

"Amazing," I said. I looked over at Mickey and saw that he still seemed to be occupied with his Black Forest cake. At least he was concentrating on the important things. "We've heard of Atlantis and other lost cities, why have we never heard of *Goren*?" I asked.

Orlando eased back in his chair, getting comfortable like someone at a picnic with friends. I guess next he'd be handing out the hot dogs for the weenie roast.

"Unfortunately, a flood destroyed the civilization and forced it to the bottom of the Pacific. I've spent years trying to locate the exact area where Goren might have been located. I thought I'd found it and sent my divers down there. However, after weeks of searching––no artifacts. Then one day, I ran into a diver—Armando. He showed me the bone, technically called, a *Riva*. The people made them to honor the gods.

I bought it from Armando and asked where he'd found it. He gave me the coordinates and I had my divers see what else they could discover there. Voila, we found several items that indicated we were in the right spot. Armando decided to work with us, but he never showed up. A week later, his dead body washed onto the shore."

I stared at Orlando for a moment, looking for any indication of guilt.

Orlando stared back. "If you're thinking I had something to do with it, you're wrong. Armando would have been useful to me in finding other treasures. So I certainly wouldn't have had him killed."

Mickey looked up from his cake, transfixed for a moment, then dug in again. He had good concentration, just not apparently for anything other than dessert.

"I finally located several more artifacts, but none as interesting as the bone. Still, I had that one. I talked to a few experts who informed me of its great value.

Stephanie found a man in Sweden who would pay me a rather large sum for it. But before she got a chance to complete the transaction, she was...murdered—and the bone stolen. I'm not sure if the same man did both, but I have a good idea who took it."

The color drained from Mickey's face. He pushed the cake away and seemed to take an active interest in the conversation. "Are you sure? I mean, I know when things are stolen from me, I really don't have a clue who's taken them. It's really hard to pin it down." He chuckled nervously.

"I know who it is." He grunted, stepping closer to Mickey. "And I'll make sure he's punished for it."

Chapter Fifty-Six

Orlando picked up Mickey's licked-clean plate and threw it against the wall. The remnants of his *dry* chicken splattered, creating a nice mural. If you're that way about art done with fowl.

Mickey shuddered, closed his eyes. Orlando approached, arms outstretched, looking like a monster, ready to tear him in two. "And when I find Victor, I will strangle him."

Mickey's eyes slowly opened. "Victor?"

Orlando's hands dropped to his sides, seeming to have forgotten all about that "tearing things in two" thing. "Yes, Victor Rawlings. He will stop at nothing to get what he wants. I believe he took the artifact...maybe killed Stephanie."

Mickey slumped in his chair, still looking pale.

"Perhaps I can use your assistance, Mr. Katz. Bring the object and Victor to me. I will take care of him in my own way."

Mickey sat up, now appearing bold. He really should look into those mood swings. "Arnie would be glad to do that for you. Wouldn't you, Arn?" He turned to me, nodding, indicating he'd like me to nod too.

What the hell was Mickey doing? "No problem getting you the bone. But I don't know about bringing in Victor."

"I'm afraid it's a package deal. Otherwise, what do I need you two alive for?"

Mickey whispered in my ear. I couldn't make out what he said, but then he moved his head closer to Orlando. "Arnie accepts."

Before I could say anything, the word *splendid* flew from Orlando's mouth. "You will receive your fifty grand when you bring Victor and the bone to me."

I said, "Great," meaning what did Mickey get me into?

Mickey said, "Wonderful," meaning let's have more cake.

I asked Orlando where Victor might be located. He had no idea. How much better could this get?

A few moments later, we were outside—Andre escorting Mickey and me out of the gate. Oddly enough, he didn't seem all that sad to see us go. I guess he kept it all inside.

On the drive back, I gave it to Mickey. "What the hell are you doing telling him that we would bring back Victor? Remember, we just went there to gather information and say that we would find the bone for him. Nothing else."

"Well we are returning the bone. And we did do some pretty heavy duty information gathering. Now we know that Victor is behind everything."

"Maybe. But you're forgetting one little detail—we have no clue what Victor looks like and where to find him."

He patted me on the shoulder. "I have confidence you'll be able to track him down."

"Thanks. But if I'm going to look for him, you're coming too. And, by the way, you'd better get that bone ready to be give back to Orlando."

I looked back at Mickey, and noticed the bone was clipped to his tie clasp.

"You know, I'm, uh, having second thoughts about that part."

Chapter Fifty-Seven

We got back a few hours later. I dropped Mickey at his place, not staying to hear all the fun Joe had dressing up as the 'horny gorilla' for that party.

I went home and sat in front of my TV watching, "Don't Hurt Them While They're Alive." I know it sounds like a horror movie, but actually it was a documentary about taking care of your teeth. I guess they have to do something special these days to capture your interest in a movie about oral health. In the middle of the most exciting part where the dentist had to extract a tooth from a 70-year-old man's mouth, there was a knock at my door.

The woman was gorgeous. Low-cut blue blouse, short pink skirt showing off her sculptured legs. Long blonde hair curled around her face like a gold frame around a painting. She looked like she could have been Miss June, or July or any month she wanted. Hell, they could make up a new month called Smiddleydo for her.

"Hi, I'm Christy Leblanc," she said in a college-girl sweet voice. "Are you Arnie Katz?"

"Yes."

"Can I come in? I have something for you."

"You didn't ring up from downstairs. At least, I didn't hear the buzzer."

"Your landlord, Mr. "Renfew, was kind enough to let me in."

That was odd. Renfew was very suspicious of everyone. I'd been living here for ten years and he still made me show him ID. Christy comes to the door and she's in.

"What's this about?"

"I'm from Corral City College." She gave me a happy face smile like they invented it for her. "It might be better if we could talk inside."

I didn't have a clue what she wanted. Maybe they heard about my speech at the dental association and wanted me to give an inspirational talk. I could do that. Maybe, 'Floss Your Way to Success." I'd have to work on that. "Yeah, sure, come on in, Christy."

She ambled in and sat on the couch in my living room. With her great-looking legs, I'm sure today, Humphrey, had his head completely out of his shell.

She opened her briefcase and removed some papers and carefully placed them on my coffee table. Then she looked up at me, showing a smile that looked like it was battery powered.

"Dean Feinstein wanted to talk to you about your program."

"My program?"

What was she talking about?

She began searching through her sheets, then found one that she seemed to favor over the others. She put the rest back into her briefcase. "Yes, the one you applied to."

"I didn't apply to any..."

She tapped the sheet, making a crinkling sound. "I have your application right here. "You know, for our legal program."

"Legal pro..." Then it hit me. Dad! He must have applied to the legal program—in my name. Unbelievable!

"It seems you didn't fill out some of the questions and I thought we could do that now."

"Just curious, Christy. Did I sign it?"

She looked at one of her sheets.

"Yes, you did." She showed me the paper with my name. Only it wasn't my signature.

This was getting more interesting. "Do you often come out to see people who miss things on the application?"

"No, not usually, but Dean Feinstein said to come because, in his words, 'you are a very special student.'"

"Thank you." I didn't think the reason was that I was special. It was probably as a favor to his old drinking buddy, my dad. I remembered dad used to tell me stories about old 'Twelve Beer' Feinstein. How on one Christmas night, the two of them got so drunk, they ended up stuck in their fraternity house chimney.

Dad had probably told the dean to get the prettiest recruiter on staff to come and see me. I'm sure he thought that would work better than mind control drugs.

"I see here by your comment that you've been in another field for a few years and you feel you've made a mistake. Nothing to be ashamed of. We all make mistakes." She smiled a cute Miss July smile.

"Actually, I never signed that."

She stared at me puzzled. "What do you mean?"

"I mean I never wanted to go to law school and I never signed that sheet."

She continued to stare.

"It's a forgery. And if I were you I'd look into the man who did it. Isn't that a felony?"

She seemed to give that some consideration. "Yes, I suppose it is." She didn't quite know what to do with that. "You sure?"

I nodded.

"I'm terribly sorry. I'll definitely look into it." She packed up her things and left, saying things like, "sorry to bother you," and a few other words that she mumbled under her breath.

I got back to my documentary.

An hour later, the phone rang. I thought it might be dad wanting me to testify at his forgery trial as a character witness. The call, however, turned out to be from Debbie, her voice tense.

"I think I'm being followed."

Chapter Fifty-Eight

"Who's following you, Debbie?"

"I don't know. Can you come over?"

I drove over to her place as quickly as my four-cylinder engine could take me. She opened the door and she wrapped her arms around me.

"It's okay, honey."

She released me and we sat down on the couch.

"Do you think it could be the police?" she asked.

"I don't think so. I already talked to Rick. After the stunt he pulled, he wouldn't do something like this without telling me."

A single tear rolled down her cheek. It looked lonely. "Look, Debbie, it's okay, everything's gonna be fine. We'll find out exactly what's going on."

Her eyes lit up. "Yes! You and me working together again."

"I don't think so. Actually, I'm working with someone else right now."

Her eyebrows seemed to raise four inches above her forehead. "You hate working with other people. Who is it?"

"That's not important."

She gave me the look that said I'd better tell her or she'd hound me about it for the rest of my life, even after I died. I took a deep breath. "Mickey."

I could feel something building up inside of her. Like a volcano before the lava spills out and destroys everything and everyone in its path.

"You're working with the guy who dumped me. How loyal of you."

"I thought you were okay with Mickey."

"I've been doing some thinking."

Oh no. That wasn't good. Debbie thinking could cause that volcano to erupt at any moment and lead to the ruin of civilization as we know it.

I decided I had to interrupt her brain activity while her neurons were still in the information-gathering phase.

"Listen, Mickey got me involved in some intricate situations, and I thought it best we work together."

She blew out air. It didn't look like she blew out any of her *angry*, but when she spoke, she wasn't that volcano anymore.

"I guess I understand. These are extraordinary circumstances."

"You got that right, Deb." I patted her shoulder. "These people who are following you, do you have any idea what they look like?"

She shook her head.

"Maybe we should get the police involved. I'm gonna talk to Rick, see if he'll send some undercover guys to watch you."

A sour expression drifted onto her face. "You know I hate being watched."

I blew out air. "Alright. Then make sure you only go out during the day and that you have someone with you at all times."

She tapped her foot on the ground, nodded. "Okay."

"Good."

"Listen, I'm sorry I bit your head off before, Arn. I'm just a little worried." She opened her eyes wide. "Are we okay?"

I smiled. "We'll always be okay."

She smiled back and grabbed my hand.

Chapter Fifty-Nine

The next day, someone else grabbed my hand—Tanya. She dragged me into the back room to tell me how 'not okay' I was.

"Where have you been?"

"Busy with a case."

"Yeah, well you have a dental practice too. Remember that? Dr. Michaels is doing what he can, but they all want to see you. I had to say you were under the weather to explain why you weren't here yesterday."

I gave her my vulnerable look where I lower my face and show her puppy dog eyes. "Sorry."

"Don't give me your vulnerable look. It's not gonna work this time."

I guess I needed a new look.

"There were at least ten people here yesterday who said they wanted to wait for you. I said I didn't know if you were coming back. They said, 'that's okay; we'll wait anyway.' Finally, at eight, when Dr. Michaels finished the ones who would see him, I pretended to call security to get the rest out of here."

"So, I'm guessing that didn't make you a happy camper?" I said, joking, trying to lighten the mood.

"Don't try and lighten the mood."

She'd figured out all my tricks. "Listen, Tanya, I've been trying to help Debbie. Right now, she's the only person the police have for Stephanie's murder. If I don't find out who the killer really is, she's gonna go back to jail...for a long time."

Her face softened. "Oh, I didn't realize."

"Okay, so let's get this day moving. Who's my first patient?"

A sinister expression appeared on her face and, immediately, I knew who it was.

I expected Nathan to be annoying as usual. But actually he behaved. Perhaps, he'd matured, seeing me as the giant of my profession that I am. Maybe, he now had a new respect for my dental skills. But in all probability, it was the horse needles I borrowed from a veterinarian friend that I laid out on my tray. They were over a foot long. Nathan's eyes didn't leave them. Of course, it didn't stop the questions, but I had an innovative way of dealing with those—cotton balls. I just couldn't decide if they should go in my ears or Nathan's mouth.

On my lunch-break, I decided to do research on Victor Rawlings. I just hoped he wasn't one of Stephanie's boyfriends too. Everyone else seemed to be. I headed down to the police station and saw Rick.

I found him sitting at his desk, staring at something wrapped in aluminum foil in front of him.

"Katz, what's up?"

"I just wanted some…"

He began opening up the foil. I smelled something that was a cross between a dead animal and another dead animal. "What the heck is that?" I asked.

"Maria in depositions made it. I think it used to be food. I'm just deciding if I want to eat it or live. Last time she brought something in I had stomach pains for a week."

Just then the lovely Maria Dixon entered the office wearing a white halter top that was so tight, it must have affected her blood pressure. I know it affected mine. She had on blue jeans and black boots. Her sexy walk made me think I wouldn't mind getting patted down by her. "Hey, Rick," she said, smiling, "Did you try it yet?"

Rick grinned back at her. "Yeah, and, truthfully, it's the best thing you've ever made."

She was on cloud nine, on her way to cloud ten. "That's great. It's a new recipe."

"I was just about to give some to Arnie." He picked up the aluminum foil and offered it to me. The closer it got to my nose, the worse it smelled. But I looked at Maria, smiling, waiting for my verdict, and couldn't refuse. I just hoped that this wasn't the way it would all end for me.

I took the fork off the plate and scooped a bit out. I chewed, chewed again, then again. Finally, I got it down. I sort of felt I should warn my stomach what was coming, but why should I? It never warned me gas was coming.

I'm a stickler for honesty, so I immediately told Maria the cold hard truth about how I felt about her creation. "Delicious."

Rick gave me a devilish smile, then turned toward Maria. "Have you given it to Sid yet?"

She shook her head. "I wanted to see what you guys thought of it first."

"Make sure you serve it tonight. I don't think he'll ever forget it."

She smiled a forty-two-teeth-baring smile. "Tonight it is!"

She left, and I stared at Rick. "How can you destroy the woman's marriage like that? Not to mention several of my internal organs."

"Actually, I think this will keep her marriage together. Sid's a chief. After he tastes this, he'll start making all the meals."

I nodded. Made sense, I guess.

"So what do you want, Arn? I'm busy."

I sat down. "I need to know anything you have on Victor Rawlings."

He looked like three-hundred volts of electricity had just been administered to his brain. "Isn't he a little out of your league?"

"What do you mean?"

"What I mean—" he said, as he lifted his legs and threw them onto his desk—is that he's a pretty rough character. To the outside world, he's a businessman, imports, exports. But we know he's involved in much more than that. There have been several murders that we're pretty confident he's had something to do with. But we just haven't been able to pin anything on him."

"Do you know where he is?"

"Not sure. But the latest info is that he's involved in some kind of undersea exploration."

My brain screamed out—him too?

"So why do you want to know about Victor?"

"I have a feeling he's the one who murdered Stephanie Warrick. Perhaps others."

A compassionate expression formed on his face. "Look, I know you want to help your friend, but despite what she's told you, did you ever think that she might actually be guilty?"

That hit me hard. At first, I thought, what's he saying? But maybe he had a point. I so desperately wanted to believe Debbie had nothing to do with any of this that I couldn't see the evidence against her clearly. She had seen Stephanie the night of the murder. She'd been very angry about Mickey. And I hadn't heard from her for a while when she suddenly popped into my office with the news about her wedding. People do change sometimes and, on occasion, it's not for the better. Had all of this been a set up by her? I considered that for a moment, feeling bad for even thinking all this.

"Listen, Rick," I said, rising from my chair, "I agree it's possible Debbie killed Stephanie. She was upset with Mickey. But I thought we already agreed she couldn't be the Orthodontist Killer."

He shrugged, picked up a file, started reading.

I decided to go another way. "Did you know that Orlando and Stephanie were an item?"

He stared at me a moment, then threw the file onto the desk, and jumped up. No longer Mr. Relaxation, more like Mr. Wild and Crazy. "They were?"

"Yes."

"That is surprising." Rick moved his body forward stiffly, as if he was a reluctant puppet. "Listen, Arnie, I can't do much for you. While we may have bits and pieces of evidence showing Orlando has been involved in nefarious activities, Victor is different. Yes, we have a file on supposed crimes committed by him, but we have no outright proof. And no pictures. No one can verify what he actually looks like. We believe he's killed for no reason. Some would say he's a psychopath.

Chapter Sixty

I left Rick's office concerned. Rick knew bad guys and he thought Victor was rougher than most. Not good. Worse yet, I'd already promised Orlando that I'd bring Victor to him and I didn't have a clue where to find him.

I decided I would ask the one person who might know something. An hour later, I sat in Benny's office, alone once again. Things in the lawyer-snitch business were really booming.

When Benny exited his office, he had another woman with him. This one, like the last was a blonde and he adjusted her blouse on leaving the office. Perhaps Benny offered a blouse-fitting service.

He made a move to kiss her, but then he noticed me and his face got that perturbed expression again. The kissing manoeuvre stopped mid-pucker.

Maybe I should work for Planned Parenthood.

He didn't even bother shaking her hand this time, just sent her away. Then he reluctantly invited me into his office. We sat down and he drank from the coffee mug sitting on his desk. I'm not exactly sure it was coffee because right after, he seemed to loosen up, smile more. He even laughed a few times.

"Boy, you must really like me, Katz. You come here so often. Is it my magnetic personality or are you trying to find out who my tailor is?"

"I need information." I laid a fifty on his desk. He didn't move for a moment, just kept his eyes on the fifty as if he were afraid it might change its mind and come back to me. It might have. I have a way with fifties. Then he scooped it up with his hand and sat back.

"What do you want to know?"

"Tell me about Victor Rawlings."

He seemed dazed for a moment, like he was unconscious and someone just gave him mouth to mouth, only the oxygen hadn't reached his brain yet.

"Why do you always come to me with the tough ones, Katz? It couldn't be someone easy like Joe Marco, the guy who robbed all those banks on the east side."

"Sorry."

He adjusted himself in his chair. "Okay, some years back, Victor and Orlando were partners in a sea exploration business. They'd find artifacts in the ocean, then try to locate people to buy them. They were doing well, made hundreds of thousands of dollars dealing with foreign buyers. The problem was they argued constantly and became mortal enemies."

"Do you think it's possible Victor killed the Warwick woman?"

He shrugged, ruining the delicate line of the already wrinkled fabric of his polyester suit. "I'm not sure. He's certainly a rough enough character to do it. But it's also possible that my car is a Rolls instead of an '82 Dodge Dart missing a door."

"Do you know where he's located?"

"I heard he lives on a boat down at the docks."

"Do you know what he looks like?"

He shrugged again. More polyester wrinkles. "That's the problem. No one does."

I thought about what Benny had told me. He was probably right about most things. But I had a hunch there was someone who knew what Victor looked like. Someone I knew.

Chapter Sixty-One

I sat on Mickey's couch while he fidgeted, walked back and forth and grimaced. I wasn't sure if he was thinking or auditioning for *West Side Story.*

He sidled up to me. "Okay, I know about Victor, but I haven't seen him in a while. He might look different."

"How long ago did you see him?"

He clicked his tongue. I had a hunch that might be Mickey's only musical talent. "Two weeks. But, you know, Arn, sometimes people change in a short period of time. Take you, for example. Last time I saw you, you were bald and had a goatee."

"I look the same as I always have."

"Maybe it's the lighting."

I headed toward the door. "I have to get going. But I want you to come down with me to the docks tomorrow and identify Victor."

"I can't. If he sees me—"

"Don't tell me you borrowed money from him too."

"No. But he and Orlando used to work together and I don't want to take chances."

I stopped at the door. "He won't see you. We'll be in my car. I'm going to take some pictures of him with my telephoto lens."

He shrugged. "Why?"

"Maybe if I show them to the police, they'll be able to match him up to crimes that have been committed. We'll have more leverage that way."

He zoned out for a moment, his mind, I'm sure, calculating how to get out of this. "I don't want to involve the police."

"It'll be fine"

His whole body seemed to collapse. Finally, in a small voice, one word dribbled out. "Okay."

"Alright, tomorrow morning. I'll pick you up about eight."

That evening, I went home and listened to some classical music—Mozart's *Symphony #14 in A Major*. As usual, the kid in the apartment above played some heavy metal from his favorite band 'Dirty Pond Scum.' Oddly enough, the combination blended well together. Although, I'm sure it would make Mozart want to throw himself in front of a bus.

I thought about what Mickey and I were doing tomorrow and my stomach tightened. Rick's comments about Victor had gotten to me.

I don't know why. I mean we were just going to take some pictures and we'd be quite a distance from the bad guys. I guess I just worried something could go wrong. But I didn't have much time to think about that as Debbie buzzed my apartment. I let her in.

"What's wrong, Debbie?"

"I've got trouble."

She sat down on the couch, her hands closed into fists.

She looked adorable—a white and red blouse, short skirt and black pumps. If she hadn't started crying, you might think she resembled a movie star. With the tears, she resembled a movie star who'd just been told she'd only get two million instead of three for a picture.

"Arnie, they followed me again."

"Where?"

"Evanston Park."

"You were with someone, right?"

"Uh, yeah, sure."

"Who?"

She tilted her head as if it weighed more on one side than the other. "Candy."

I raised my eyebrow. Just the right one. The other one was beat. "Who's she?"

"My next door neighbor's dog."

"Deb, when I said don't go out alone, I meant for you to be with someone of the human species."

"Yeah, well, uh, Emily's on holiday and asked me to look after Candy for a few days. She can be quite aggressive if need be. You should see the way she tosses her NERF ball around."

"Sounds pretty terrifying."

"Anyway, yesterday was fine. We did our walk, then came home. But today on the way to the park, I could feel someone's eyes on me. I checked around, didn't see anyone. So I thought maybe I've been imagining all this. But then, Candy started growling and I saw a man stare at me for an instant, then he seemed to disappear into the crowd."

"Did you get a look at him?

"Yes. He was either a fat bald guy, a short man with big ears, or a woman with blue hair."

"You've really narrowed it down, Deb."

She gave me a look that said don't push it. So instantly, using my razor sharp mental powers I figured out that maybe I shouldn't push it.

"Candy and I ran all the way home. I left her there with some chew toys and came straight over to see you. I'm so paranoid I went out by the back door and looked behind me several times."

More tears came and she threw her arms around me.

"Don't worry, everything will be okay." I said it with enough force that I almost believed it.

Chapter Sixty-Two

"Can I stay here tonight?"

I looked at Debbie's sad face. I didn't really think it would be a good idea. On the other hand, it might be safer for her. "Okay. You take the bed. I'll sleep on the couch."

She looked at me. "Can we both be in the bed?"

"Okay, but just for sleep. I have to get up early tomorrow."

The next morning, I awoke about seven. I lay next to Debbie, my cheek stuck to hers like we'd been crazy-glued together. We probably could have gotten a job in the sideshow as Siamese Twins.

I carefully pulled my cheek off hers and got up. I thought I'd let her sleep a little longer. I went to the kitchen and made breakfast for both of us.

It felt strange being in bed together and not involving ourselves in any extracurricular activities. But it was for the best. Maybe we could, at least, talk about seeing each other after we got her off the police radar, so to speak.

I went back to the bedroom. She looked very peaceful. I hated to wake her, but I had to leave. I prodded her shoulder and her eyes fluttered.

I knew I'd have to make up some excuse about my destination, some place she wouldn't want to go. Otherwise, she might try to tag along.

She opened her eyes wide. "The Morgue? You're going to the Morgue?"

"Yeah, it's for one of my cases."

"Sounds scary."

"Yeah," I said. "It does. It is. One of my clients thinks someone replaced his uncle's body with another corpse. And he's afraid if he checks, he might be seen. So he asked me to do it for him." Where do I come up with them? Maybe too much green tea.

"Interesting."

"Listen, Debbie, you can stay here if you want. It's probably a good idea. I called Rick last night and arranged for him to assign an undercover policeman to watch you."

Debbie sighed.

"I know you don't like being watched. But please, for my piece of mind, do this."

Her eyes slowly moved right, as if they were snails on Valium. "Okay."

"If you want to go out, I'll give you the cell number of the undercover guy. Get him to come along. I don't want you going out alone, understand?"

"Yeah, yeah."

I gave her my stern look. "I mean it. If someone's truly following you, we're into a dangerous situation."

"I know."

"I made breakfast for you."

"Thanks, Arn." She kissed me and I left.

I picked up Mickey at his apartment and we headed down to the docks. We parked in a vacant lot near the water so we'd have a clear view of the ships.

Mickey took a falafel out of a bag and started eating—most of the chick peas oozing out onto the floor of my recently detailed car.

"Can you try to be less messy?"

Mickey spread his hands. "Arnie, the falafel is meant to be eaten messy."

Of course, I'd seen Mickey at meals before and had a feeling he believed every food group should be eaten messy. Somehow he made a mess eating a grape.

I picked up my binoculars and could see a dinghy docked at shore. Two men were arguing. I handed the binocs to Mickey.

He looked through them, shook his head. "Don't see Victor, but I do see the guy who had the gun on us at Orlando's."

"Adrian? That's odd," I said. "Orlando hates Victor, yet the same man is working for both of them. Doesn't make sense."

I took the binoculars back, wiping the chick pea sauce from them. Mickey took another bite of his lunch. From what I could understand from his pita-filled mouth, he said, "It's stupid to stay here. Most criminals do their evil deeds at night."

"Let's wait a little while longer and see what happens."

Mickey looked at me none too happy. "I have things to do, Arnie."

"What things?"

"I'd rather not get into them right now. But, uh, important meetings with, uh, important people."

I stared at his chick-pea-sauce-filled face and, of course, knew that a man like him would have lots of appointments.

We sat there a while, Mickey eating, me looking through the binoculars every once in a while. Nothing much changed and I was beginning to think this had been a colossal waste of time.

I looked through the binoculars once more and noticed a large, swarthy man standing beside Adrian. I quickly handed the binoculars to Mickey. "Is that Victor?"

"Yeah, that's him."

I pulled out my camera and snapped shots of the two men. Unfortunately, as I looked through the viewfinder of the camera, Adrian looked right back at me. The next thing I knew, he'd left the dinghy and had started running toward us.

Mickey screamed. "Drive Arnie, drive!"

Chapter Sixty-Three

I drove fast down side streets back to Mickey's apartment, not noticing anyone following us. When we got inside, Mickey sat down on the couch and hyperventilated, his face white and sweaty. On him it looked kind of natural. I ambled into Mickey's small office, hooked up my camera to his computer and printed up the pictures.

I went back into the living room and placed the photos on the coffee table. I sat down on the couch beside Mickey, his face still pale. He turned to me. "Why did I ever let you talk me into this?"

"You wanted to help Debbie, remember? You said it's the least you could do."

"Well, that didn't include getting killed. Now that they've seen us, who knows what's going to happen. They could come here in the middle of the night and grab me.

"I don't think they could recognize us, but the good news is we managed to get pictures of them." I pointed to the photos on the table.

"Unfortunately, no evidence."

"Not yet. Maybe we'll catch a lucky break soon."

At that moment, we both heard footsteps outside and our eyes turned in unison to the door. It slowly opened and Joe entered the room. Mickey and I relaxed. He wore no disguise and somehow that made him seem less real.

Mickey nodded toward him. "Hey, Joe, what's up? You didn't work today?"

"Nah," he grimaced. "They offered me a gig dressing up as a clown for a kid's birthday party, but you know I have standards. Of course, the fact that my feet were too big for the clown shoes had something to do with it too." He looked at the pictures on the table. "Who's that?"

Mickey started to speak. "Oh, that's..."

I jumped in. "It's just some people on a boat. Mickey thought I'd like to see some of his photography."

Joe nodded. "Good work, Mickster. They should be hanging in a gallery somewhere."

Mickey smiled, wallowing in the compliment, apparently forgetting that he had nothing to do with them and that his major artistic contribution today was spreading falafel all over the interior of my car.

Joe turned, walked into his room, closed the door.

I examined the photos again and something hit me. I handed one of them to Mickey.

"Take a look at this."

"What?"

"Adrian's wrist."

"I don't see anything."

I tapped the photo. "There."

Mickey's eyes and jaw widened, not easy to do at once. "It's the bracelet with the tiny figures that was in Stephanie's apartment."

"Yeah, but is it the same one?"

Mickey scrunched up his forehead. "Actually, there's an easy way to tell. Stephanie used to show me a scrawl in the center of the bracelet. It resembled an eye. She used to joke about it watching us."

I took out my key fob and removed the magnifying glass, handed it to Mickey. "See if it's there."

Mickey checked the photo from every conceivable angle. He bent down, turned his body to the right, moved side to side. It looked like some kind of weird aerobic exercise. I bet he lost five pounds.

He turned to me, like a school kid who'd just aced an exam. "It's there."

"Great. So that means this guy, Adrian, must have gone to Stephanie's place before you did on the night of the murder."

Mickey looked pumped as if his previous "aerobics" had done him some good. "Right, cause I was there the day before and I saw the bracelet. That means he killed Stephanie. Case solved."

"Slow down, Mickey. Right now, we have an overload of suspects at Stephanie's on the same day as the murder—him, you, Debbie."

"Well, I didn't do it. And I'm sure Debbie didn't. That really only leaves Adrian. Case solved, as I said. Debbie won't be under suspicion any longer."

"We need proof, Mickey."

"I think if they look at the three of us, they'll be able to figure out which one of us is the criminal."

I looked at Mickey and wasn't so sure about that. I knew we needed to go into surveillance mode and watch Adrian's house. Mickey was totally against the idea. But then later that night, he called me and said he'd had a change of heart. We should see Adrian. He was almost giddy about it.

Mickey happy about seeing Adrian? There was definitely something wrong with that.

Chapter Sixty-Four

I got Adrian's address from Rick at the station and then drove over to Mickey's. He sounded so happy last night that I expected him to be all ready to go. But he answered the door wearing pjs with pictures of teeth all over them and the words, 'bite me' written in big letters. He was wavering, and in his hand he grasped a bottle of Scotch. I assumed he was having misgivings about the trip.

"You're not ready," I said.

He walked over to the couch and plopped down.

"Why did I ever let her go, Arnie?" he said, his words slurred.

"Who?"

"Debbie. She's beautiful and smart and she loved me."

I looked at my watch. "I don't know. But we should get going."

He didn't get going. "I should have married her." He took a swig of scotch. "I'm gonna get her back."

I stared at him like someone looks at a dog that can't get the ball out of the bushes. "Mickey, I don't think she'll—"

He had an ear to ear grin. "Sure, she will. She loved me once. I just have to make her love me again. I'll take her away where it's just me and her and get her to change her mind. Yeah, that's it. Some faraway place."

"Mickey, we gotta get a move on."

He seemed to snap out of it. "Yeah, okay." He put the scotch down on the table and stood up with a renewed sense of energy. Then, on the way to the door he opened up a desk drawer and removed a large brown envelope. He stepped out of the house and as the brilliant sun shone on him, his energy seemed to disappear and he began yawning. It looked like he might fall onto the side-walk, head-first. That wouldn't be good for anyone, but especially for a guy like Mickey who might be down to his last three neurons. I grabbed him before he damaged those and managed to steady him on his feet. His grasp on that envelope was tight and it made me wonder what was in it. Maybe I didn't want to know.

As I helped him toward the car, I made sure Mickey didn't fall and break anything. I had a hunch a broken Mickey would be even more annoying that an in-one-piece Mickey.

Finally, I pushed him into the car and we were off. He didn't say much along the way, I presumed, since he was still out of it.

The drive to Adrian's place only took about twenty minutes. Half-way there, he seemed to sober up. He looked through the windows and asked, "Where are we going?"

"Adrian's place."

Mickey's left leg began shaking and he stuttered out the words, "Adrian's place?"

"Yeah."

Now his right leg began shaking. Play a little *Jail House Rock* and you'd think he was doing a bad Elvis impression. Or a good one. Hard to tell the difference sometimes.

"What's wrong, Mickey?"

An expression that resembled guilt covered his face. I could feel something bad coming. Just like how my aunt could sense what kind of weather we were going to have by her arthritis. Of course, she'd always be wrong.

If she said *tornado,* you'd better pick up some sun screen.

When we arrived, we parked across the road. I scanned the outside of Adrian's house and saw nothing unusual—a white picket fence, well-manicured lawn, veranda. I had a feeling there might be a trampoline in the back, although I had a hunch a bad guy like Adrian might be more of a swing kind of fellow.

Mickey moistened his lips. "Arnie, there's something I have to tell you about Adrian."

"He's dangerous, I know."

"No, something else." He looked down at his shoes, then back at...pretty well, everything—except me. "See, he called last night."

"He called? Why didn't you tell me?"

More lip moistening. "The thing is I may have been drunk then too. He told me he saw you and me with the camera the other day. And he, uh, said that if I brought the pictures to him, he'd erase my gambling debts, plus give me twenty grand for my trouble."

"Go on."

"The problem is he wanted something else too."

"What? What did he want?"

He paused a moment, then said one word. "You."

"What do you mean?" I said, gripping the steering wheel tight, my knuckles bone-white.

"He wanted me to bring you here. He said he'd take care of the rest. He said that's all I had to do."

"I see. Of course, you refused."

He stared at his shoes again. "Well, you know, Arn, I'm in kind of dire straits right now, broke and everything...did I mention I was drunk when I talked to him?"

My grip on the steering wheel intensified and I worried it might come lose. This was unbelievable. The guy I'd be trying to help, had double-crossed me. It shocked me so much that I didn't notice the moment when Adrian came over to the car and pointed his gun in our window. "Hello gentlemen."

Chapter Sixty-Five

He waved the gun around this way and that, as if it were a bird he was attempting to make fly. Then he forced me to open the car door. He slid into the back seat, still holding the gun on us. "Just sit tight while I figure out the plan."

Mickey glanced at me like he wanted to tell me some more things. After his other wonderful news about selling me out, I'm not sure I wanted to hear them. Of course, it could have been some kind of apology. But I doubt that even Emily Post knew the proper thing to say to someone after you'd sold them up the river.

A moment later, a more positive spin on this situation popped into my brain. Mickey was going to bargain with Adrian to get me out of this spot. Well done, Mickey! I felt a smile form on my lips, as he turned to our guest to begin negotiating.

"Listen, Adrian, I don't want to bother you; I see you're in the middle of something here, but could I get my money now?" He handed him the brown envelope with, I now assumed, all the pictures I'd taken. "Maybe in small bills so I don't have to go to the bank."

Adrian didn't seem to have a clue what Mickey was talking about. And Mickey, well, his mind was probably working out the details of some awesome humanitarian deed—like selling my blood to the Red Cross after Adrian shot me.

Mickey continued. "Remember, you said you'd give me twenty grand if I brought Arnie and the pictures to you. You have the pictures. He pointed toward the envelope. "And there's Arnie." He pointed toward me. "You have everything."

"Changed my mind, loser." Adrian laughed. "I think we're all going to take a little trip together. Won't that be fun? Start driving, Katz."

Mickey's pale face gradually morphed into the shade of green that turtles have during ovulation. "You know, I'm not really good on trips," I said. "I get car sick a lot."

"Can it."

Adrian tapped my neck with his cold gun. My neck shivered. "Turn right here, Katz."

I did what he asked, then we drove for about two hours, passing forests, farm houses and seeing almost every type of cow known to man. What a nightmare. I'm lactose intolerant!

Adrian grunted. "Turn on the speed. What are you? An old lady?"

I had been driving the speed limit, but if he wanted me to be faster, I was happy to oblige. I revved up the car to 80 and barrelled down the dirt road like I was at Le Mans. I hoped a cop would stop us.

No cop. Maybe it was all policed by cows.

Adrian had me drive into a large barren lot with a small yellow farm house and park. Pretty usual— thatched roof, no windows and thankfully, no cows. My stomach felt better already.

Adrian forced us out of the car and inside the farm house.

It was empty and dark. He walked us toward a small room in the back. Spots of mold covered the walls and there was straw all over the ground. He had Mickey tie me up, then he tied up Mickey. In a way, I thought that was good news. It meant that at least we weren't going to be killed.

Seconds later, I realized I might have been wrong about the killing thing when he brought out matches and poured kerosene on the straw.

He lit a match and threw it on the ground, then watched for a moment as the fire started to rage. He gagged slightly, rushed toward the door and ran out.

Smoke filled the room and Mickey and I both began to cough at the same time. For a moment, I lost sight of him as smoke created a ghostly barrier between us. I squinted through the haze and could see Mickey's head resting on his chest, his face blank, like someone had sucked the spirit right out of him.

I didn't feel so good either. The aroma of smoke filled my lungs, and every muscle in my arms and legs felt paralyzed. As I struggled to get free of the ropes, I fell onto my side and tried to manoeuvre my gingival probe out of my inside pocket.

I swivelled my body to the left until it fell from my pocket. My hands were tightly tied, but after a few tries I managed to pick the probe up with my feet, and bring it toward my hands. My fingers were able to grab hold of it and gradually loosen the ropes.

When I'd freed myself, I shoved the rope into my pocket and raced over to Mickey. I quickly undid the ropes around him. He looked out of it and I wondered if he was okay. I slapped his face and his eyes flickered so I figured he was going to be alright. I inhaled some smoke and started coughing. I moved toward the door, then kicked it down. I found a window and banged my probe against it. The window shattered and I inhaled some fresh air. I went back and picked up Mickey. Dodging the flames, I carried him across the road. As I laid him on the grass, I saw the roof of the farm house burst into flames, the entire place collapsing.

I shook Mickey a few times, but his eyes remained closed. I gave him mouth to mouth, but nothing happened. I tried one more time, then saw his chest rise and his breathing become regular. A moment later, his eyes twitched open and he said, "Am I dead?"

"No, Mickey, you're not. And I have a feeling Adrian's gonna be very disappointed about that."

"Listen, Arnie, I know I brought a lot of this down on us. I'm sorry. I wrecked your life and Debbie's. I'm gonna fix things with both of you. And I'm gonna get her back, make her love me again. He pulled the box with the bone out of his pocket. "Make sure Orlando gets this."

Chapter Sixty-Six

I drove Mickey to the hospital and had the nurses take care of him. Then I headed over to the police and explained what had happened. They filed a report and said they'd investigate when they could.

I knew I'd have to finish this off by myself. I couldn't depend on anyone else. I quickly went to my office and grabbed a few things. It was a Sunday so I wouldn't have to worry about explaining anything to Tanya.

I drove to Adrian's house. Saw his car in the driveway so I knew he had made it back from the fun times he had had with Mickey and me. Who knows, maybe he was finishing up a puzzle of *Planet of The Apes* and had one monkey to go.

I knocked at the front door. When he answered, I quickly moved behind the door so he wouldn't see me. He walked outside and looked puzzled when there was no one there. I jumped in front of him, threw a punch into his solar plexus. He dropped to the ground like an asteroid hitting the earth.

I reached down, grabbed his gun. I glanced all around to make sure no one in the neighbourhood saw what had transpired. I hate gossip.

I dragged the body inside.

For an evil side-kick, Adrian didn't have a bad place. Open kitchen concept, mood lighting. He even had a curio cabinet with old plates that might be collector's items. I pulled him over to a chair, then using all the muscles I'd developed as a dentist, forced him to sit down. He slouched, but I didn't get on him about his bad posture or anything. I pulled out the rope that he had tied around Mickey, then tied him up.

I sat in a nearby chair waiting for him to wake up. A few moments later, he did.

"Have a nice sleep, Adrian?"

He pulled on his ropes a bit. "What's going on, Katz?"

"You like games, don't you?"

"No."

"Come on, it'll be fun. I thought we'd play twenty questions. First one, did you kill Stephanie Warwick?"

He didn't say anything.

"I'd answer if I were you. You know I'm a dentist and, lucky you, I have some of my tools with me."

No words came out his mouth, so I brought my tools out from my pocket. "These are pretty sharp. I just hope I don't spill too much of your blood on the carpet."

Still no words. But he didn't look so good. I'm guessing the fact that he might bleed worried him more than messing up his carpet. Although you never know; it's damn hard to get blood stains out of shag.

"Oh, yeah, I also have something else you might be interested in." I withdrew my osteotome. I opened and closed the sharp steel blades inches from his nose. "This is used to cut into bone when I put a filling in. But I can use it to cut other things." I moved the instrument slowly down the length of his body to his crotch.

His mouth opened slightly, looking like he wanted to retch. I decided not to tell him that the *other things* I used it to cut were broccoli, carrots and rutabagas before I put them into the pot and made a nice stew.

"Let's start with the extractor." I moved it toward his mouth. Closer, closer, closer. I leaned the edge of the sharp pointy end on his upper lip. His eyes opened wide.

I didn't really want to use my instruments like this. It felt wrong somehow, like the way a butcher feels about touching a vegetarian hamburger.

I waited for Adrian to say something. Finally, he whispered, "Stop."

I pulled my instruments away from his mouth and waited.

He spoke quietly. "Yeah, I killed the Warwick woman."

"On Orlando's orders?"

He shook his head. "No."

"You're not covering for him, are you?"

"No. the command came from Victor."

"Victor?"

"Orlando sent me to get a job with Victor so that I could find out about his activities. I got deep into his organization. Eventually, he asked me to kill Stephanie to get back at Orlando. They were half-brothers and hated each other."

"So it all came down to sibling rivalry."

"Victor hated Orlando since birth because the family treated him better. They believed Orlando was good, but Victor was bad. In some ways they were right. If I had refused to do the hit I would have been a dead man. My allegiance was to Orlando, but I had no way out."

I almost felt sorry for him. He was a man caught in the middle. Still, he had pulled the trigger, taken another person's life. He had to pay. But, of course, Victor had to pay too.

I called the police. They took Adrian into custody. I gave them the picture I had of Victor and told them where to find his boat.

I had one final person to see.

Chapter Sixty-Seven

I waited in front of the wire barricade until seconds later, Orlando came out to greet me.

We walked inside his small, pristine office and I gave him the bone. He examined it from all angles.

"Very good, Mr. Katz. I'm impressed. Where is Victor?"

I drew a breath, knowing he wouldn't be pleased. "Let me explain a few things first. Adrian, under orders from Victor, killed Stephanie."

"Adrian?"

"Yes, he didn't want to, but Victor would have killed him if he didn't. Both are in jail right now, awaiting trial."

I put my hand in my pocket and grabbed hold of my carver. Who knew what Orlando would do to me? "I understand it's not what you wanted, and I don't care about the fifty grand. But I'd appreciate it if you could forgive Mickey's debts just the same."

Orlando sat down, an expression on his face that I couldn't read. "Mr. Katz, I appreciate you procuring the bone. I will forgive Mickey's debt only because of you." He reached into his coat and pulled out an envelope. "This is the fifty grand. Victor in jail is a fitting conclusion."

He shook my hand and I left Orlando, happy that everything had worked out as well as it had.

As Mickey would say, "case closed."

The first thing I did was phone Debbie at my place to tell her the good news. She didn't pick up, so I left a message letting her know that Stephanie's murderer was now behind bars and she would no longer be under suspicion. I phoned the hospital to see how Mickey was doing but he'd already been released.

When I got back to my office, I had planned to tell Tanya the whole story, but I found her sitting at the reception desk, wiping her eyes.

"What's wrong, Tany?"

"You were so right about Milton."

"Mr. Hair Weave?"

"He turned out to be a jerk, lied to me. He didn't have a house in the Hollywood Hills. He didn't have that great job." She wiped her eyes. "He was unemployed and had a whole raft of other girls he was seeing. I didn't care that he was unemployed, it's just that he lied. I'm never gonna find anyone, Arnie."

I gave her a hug. "I'm sorry, honey. But you can't let this turn you off men. You're a terrific person. I know there's someone perfect out there for you."

She swallowed hard. "Thanks, Arn, but—"

"I just don't want you to meet that Mr. Perfect too soon and leave your job here. You know I'd be lost without you."

She smiled. "You got that right."

We both laughed.

Later that day, Tanya seemed in better spirits. Maybe because she forgot about Mr. Hair Weave or perhaps due to the fact that I had phoned Leo Simpson, the guy she met at the dental convention, and said that she was now available.

He invited her out to lunch.

Another happy ending.

My next task was a bit more difficult. I had to get a happy ending in Rodrico's case. I didn't feel as confident about that.

Later that afternoon, I went to see Lucky. Robert answered the door. "I don't think Lucky wants to see you now—or ever." Then he noticed the woman I had with me.

"Who's she?"

"Lucinda. I think Lucky might want to see her."

Robert didn't quite understand, but he let us go in anyway.

Lucky's eyes, and probably a few more things, expanded, as Lucinda walked into his office wearing a bright blue pastel blouse, hot pink skirt and high black boots.

"Hey, Luck."

"Lucinda? What are you—?"

I piped in. "I thought you two would like to talk."

Lucinda stretched her hand out to Lucky. "It's been a while."

He nodded. "How have you been?"

She grinned. "Gettin' by."

She stared into his eyes, as if she were a student who had a crush on the teacher. "Look, I want you to know that Rodrico had nothing to do with us breaking up. He and I both knew we weren't right for one another. In fact, he told me to go back to you."

"He did?"

"But I couldn't go back just then. My mom got sick and I had to take care of her. That's why I didn't return any of your calls. I had to spend all my time with her."

Lucky blinked a few times. "I see."

I left the room and let the two of them talk. I walked into what looked like a small library down the hall. All kinds of books. I picked out one on abnormal psychology. When I finished the first page, I realized that I worked with a lot of these people.

Ten minutes later, I went back to see Lucky and Lucinda. They were sitting beside one another like two teenagers with a crush on each other.

Lucky stood up and gangster-walked over to me. Each footstep sounded like a gunshot and by time he reached me, he seemed like a one man firing squad. I was ready for anything, but he just patted my shoulder. "Tell Rodrico, we're all clear. If he wants to arrange a meeting between us, that would be okay with me. I think we could work things out."

I nodded. "Great."

Lucinda and Lucky smiled at one another and it seemed as if they might have a future together.

That's me, Arnie Katz, PI, dentist and relationship expert. Except, that is, with my own relationships.

I left with the good vibes dancing in my head and drove over to see Rodrico. I told him the good news and he beamed.

"Great job, my friend. I want to remind you that you're family. And family takes care of family. Anytime I can do anything for you, anything at all, just let me know."

I thanked him, thinking I wouldn't ever take him up on that.

But I was wrong.

Chapter Sixty-Eight

I went home to my place. Debbie wasn't there, but the bed had been made and the room cleaned up. She even left a mint on the pillow. It was an inside joke between the two of us. She used to get upset with me when things weren't neat and say, "I'm not a maid, Arnie." I'd tell her, "I know that. Things would be much cleaner if you were." She'd laugh and forgot that she was upset.

I phoned her cell. No answer. *That's odd,* I thought, but then I remembered she'd told me about some trouble with her phone lately. So I wasn't that concerned.

I decided to check with the undercover agent that Rick had following her. I called his phone. Again, no answer.

I couldn't believe it. In this age of super technology, we're all supposed to be connected twenty-four/seven and I couldn't get anyone on the line.

I left a message there too. I decided to phone the operator and ask if any calls had been made on my land line and to whom. I wanted to see if Debbie had called the undercover guy. The operator told me that the phone hadn't been used.

She wasn't here and I had told her to contact the undercover guy if she went out. That got me worried, but then a few moments later, my land line rang. I hoped it was Debbie.

"Mr. Katz?"

"Yes?"

"It's Sid Barton; I'm the undercover cop who—"

"Right."

"There's a, uh, bit of a problem. Miss Walters left this afternoon and I followed her. But it almost seemed like she was trying to lose me. She zigzagged all over the city. First, she went to Evanston Park, which is on the east side. Then she headed to the Allen Mall which is in the west. That's where I lost her. I'm sorry."

"It's not your fault. She doesn't like being watched. But we've got to find her as soon as we can."

"I'm on it."

"Why don't you go back to the Allen Mall and check again," I said. "I'll go to her apartment and see if any of the neighbors have seen her."

"Great."

I headed to 83 Wintergarden, Debbie's place and buzzed her apartment. No answer. A man came out of the building, and I walked in. I took the elevator up and was about to knock on Debbie's door when I ran into her neighbor, Ida Liebman, carrying a laundry basket. "She's not there, Arnie."

"Have you seen here lately?"

"Yeah, today. Are you two getting back together? You were such a nice couple."

"I don't know, Ida. What time did you see her?"

She lowered her head, moved close to me. "That sounds like a *no*. She's a beautiful girl, maybe you should try harder. I like you much better than that other guy." She started to walk back to her apartment.

"What other guy?"

She turned back to face me, but remained in the same spot. "I came by earlier to give Debbie some muffins I'd baked. She was just leaving her apartment, wearing this lovely white and blue laced blouse. It looked so nice. A man was with her. He seemed to be pushing her, you know, forceful. I didn't like him."

"What did he look like?"

"Well, let's see. He was tall, had a suit on. But it didn't look good on him. Like he wasn't used to wearing things like that—awkward...not a friendly face."

"Did you hear where they were going?"

"No, sorry." She glared at me. "If you want her back you gotta fight for her."

"Thanks, Ida."

A moment later, she disappeared, not knowing what devastating news she'd just given me.

Chapter Sixty-Nine

I walked over to Debbie's apartment. She had given me a key when we were going out and I'd forgotten to return it. Maybe on purpose.

I opened the door expecting to see an apartment that had been searched and left dishevelled. But it seemed as if Debbie had just hired a cleaning lady this morning— floors gleaming, carpet vacuumed. Everything in its place. Obviously, whoever took her wasn't looking for any object in the apartment. They just wanted her.

But why?

I headed down to police headquarters to see Rick. I told him the story and waited, hoping he had the answers.

He thought for a moment, then looked at me with bloodshot eyes. "I'm sorry, Katz, but I think we're out of luck here. You have no leads as to who could have done this." He turned his palms upward. "I have no leads."

I didn't know what to say. I thought he'd have some ideas. I sat there, not having the will or energy to get up.

A moment later, John, one of Rick's officers sauntered in wearing jeans and a blue shirt. John and I had worked together before on a few cases. Good guy. He carried a thick file folder in his hand. "Got some information on the orthodontist case, chief." He saw me, nodded. "Sorry, Arnie, didn't know you were here."

"It's okay. You guys go ahead."

I tried to give them their privacy by walking over to the bulletin board on the wall and studying the police sketch of the Orthodontist Killer. As much as I tried not to listen to what Rick and John were talking about, I heard every word. It's a private detective's curse— you're always listening.

"Forensics did a thorough examination of that last victim's house and found traces of this."

I shifted around and pretended to look out the window, but I saw John remove a test tube from his pocket and hand it to Rick. "It's some kind of wax. We don't know what type as yet. But they're examining it in the lab."

"Wax? That's all you got?"

"Sorry, chief."

John left and Rick muttered something to himself. I could see by the new lines forming on his face that this case had really aged him.

I sauntered over. We talked a bit more about Debbie and he said if he heard anything he'd let me know. I had no clue what to do next. I'd never felt so hopeless before.

That evening, I didn't sleep much. I spent most of the night wracking my brain trying to come up with some way I could track down Debbie. Nothing came to mind.

The next morning, I had patients to see but I didn't feel like going in. I phoned Tanya and told her to have Dr. Michaels look after them for me.

"Why?" she asked.

"I just don't think I'd be at my best."

"You get in here now, Arnie Katz! It's crazy today. Some patients have appointments, some have been waiting since we opened."

"Maybe tomorrow."

"Arnie, it's too much just for Dr. Michaels."

"But—"

"Mrs. Dowd says she wants you to fix the tooth she broke playing in her all-cougar volleyball game and Mr. Simmons said basically the same thing, except for the cougar part."

I could hear Tanya had her old spunk back. I guess Leo had worked his magic.

"Alright, I'll be there soon."

When I got to the office, I could see there was another SRO crowd. Normally, I'd be able to handle it. But today, I didn't have the strength. Nothing meant anything. I didn't even care about the free Danishes the guy with the cart gave me every day. And he had blueberry.

I told Tim that we'd split up the patients. Of course, as always, he smiled. Then I hesitantly walked into my office and prepared for the day. Tanya followed. I guess she could see something was off. She grabbed my hand and pulled me into the back room.

"What's wrong, Arnie?"

"Nothing."

She looked at me like Superman when he uses his x-ray vision. Only her powers go deeper. "I can tell when you're upset."

"It's just I promised Debbie I'd protect her and now I have no clue where she is or even if she's still..."

She looked into my eyes and maybe into my soul. "Look, Arn, I know you feel down now. But you've been through a lot of cases and you've solved them, saved people's lives sometimes. I know in my heart you'll solve this one too and Debbie will be fine."

I nodded, even though I didn't feel her confidence. I went into work. My first patient was...the Slatsky Kid.

"How come you look so sad, Doctor Katz?"

I guess I couldn't hide how I felt, even from him. I knelt down so I could look him in the eye. "Nathan, have you ever lost something that you loved?"

"Sure. I once couldn't find my favorite video game—*Demons of The Dead*." I looked everywhere. My dad eventually bought me another one.

"How did you feel when you lost it?"

"Worst day of my life."

"Well, today is like the worst day of my life. Someone is in trouble and I don't know how to help them."

He looked at me a moment, like he was analyzing things, trying to understand. "If you want I'll let you play with my *Demons of The Dead*. That always makes me feel better."

I smiled for the first time in a long while, touched. "Thanks a lot, Nathan. That helped." I patted him on the head.

I cleaned his teeth and he left. I had one last patient to see. A new one—Mrs. Sharon Lancaster. Usually with new patients, I began by joking to make them comfortable. Today, I couldn't do it.

I looked in her mouth and saw several crooked upper molars, two of them almost protruding outside her mouth. It was the worst malocclusion I'd ever seen. "Mrs. Lancaster, can you open and close your mouth a few times for me?" She did and I could see it was even worse than I'd thought.

"Do you get headaches or pains in your upper jaw?"

Her eyebrows shot up. "How did you know?"

"It's your bite. It's so irregular it's causing pressure on your jaw muscles and that's also affecting the nerves all the way up to your head."

"Can you help me?"

Despite my distaste for certain other dental professionals, those professionals were probably her only hope. "You need to see an orthodontist. If you don't, you could end up losing your teeth and it might affect your health in other ways."

Her eyes moistened. "I'm afraid to go with all those killings. Can't you please help me?"

I told her I'd see what I could do, but I didn't think I was up to the challenge. I booked her in for next week, hoping I'd figure out something by then.

Chapter Seventy

After she left, I told Tanya I had to go to the dental library at Corral University. Tanya wasn't happy about me leaving, but I explained that it was important and I'd be back soon.

I parked in the lot and walked up the laneway. CU still looked the same as always—the big white buildings with numerous tiny windows, the oak trees rising up from the very green grass, the students carrying backpacks of books trying to make it to their next class on time.

Once in the Curtis Library, I inhaled the delicious aroma of old books and magazines. I used to be addicted to that smell. Maybe that explains why I spent so much time here. That and no dates. Hard to believe as it sounds, there weren't any 'dental groupies.'

I went through two sets of doors and headed to the area where they housed specialized books on dentistry and related fields. A thirty-ish girl wearing red-tinged glasses sat behind a desk reading a book. Streaks of blonde littered her otherwise mousy brown hair. I looked at the name plate on the desk. "Excuse me, Gloria."

Her head popped up like a jack in the box, "Hi. Can I help?" she said, closing her book.

I looked at the cover. *Enhancement Orthodontics: Theory and Practice.* "Well, first of all, you don't need any enhancements anywhere."

She blushed, then laughed.

"Sorry, couldn't help it." I smiled. "Where would I find books on orthodontics?"

She pointed over to a section in the corner. "There. Were you looking for anything special?"

"Yes, malocclusion."

She stared at me for a moment, then seeming to make up her mind about something, began typing on her computer. "We have eight books, four are out right now. but the rest should be there. Let me write down their numbers."

A moment later, she handed me a piece of paper with the titles.

"Thanks; I appreciate it."

"Oh, wait a sec, I forgot something." She reached out her small hand and I handed her the paper back. She wrote something on the other side. "You might need this."

I looked at the sheet again. It now had a phone number.

She gave me a shy smile. "I'm free Tuesday."

I grinned. "Thanks," and put it into my pocket. I didn't know what to do about that and didn't want to think about it right now.

I went to the stacks and found the four books Gloria had written down. There were only three other people in the library so I had my choice of seating accommodations. I sat at a small table in the corner.

I started reading one of the books entitled, *Practical Orthodontistry* and was enthralled. I really didn't know there was so much to the field. I began to realize that maybe orthodontists had reasons for their attitude. It wasn't easy work. Yes, dentists had tough work too, but the orthodontists needed to have more of a delicate balance between artistry and craft.

One thing I realized is that I couldn't fix Mrs. Lancaster's teeth—at least not alone. But who could I get to help? Not Mickey, that's for sure. As I thought about this, I haphazardly flipped through the book. My fingers found a section dealing with orthodontic supplies. The heading was *wax*. Wax! That was what Rick had found at the scene of the Orthodontist Killer's last murder. Did that mean that he was an orthodontist? It would explain a lot.

I went outside and phoned Rick. "I just wanted to find out if you discovered what type of wax you found at the crime scene."

A pause. "How'd you know about that?"

"Sorry, couldn't help listening in the other day."

"Arnie, this is police business."

"I believe someone else video-taped something they shouldn't have. I think that makes us even."

"Alright, you've got me on that one. No nothing new. I haven't heard back from Forensics yet. They've got a lot on their plate right now—a murder out in East York."

I hung up, disappointed. But, at that moment, I realized who could help me with Mrs. Lancaster.

"Hello, Edward, how are you doing?"

"All better. Back to teaching at the College."

"I wondered if you could recommend a good orthodontist for a patient." I described her trouble to him.

"It's been a while, but I'd be happy to do what I can."

"She's actually a little nervous about seeing an orthodontist because of the murders."

"Maybe we can work together at your office. That might make her feel better."

"I'd like that, Edward. And I think she would too. It'll be like the old days at school."

"Yes, but this time I hope you're going to suck up to the teacher."

I laughed, then hung up. Edward always had a way of making me feel better.

I decided to check back with Ida, Debbie's next door neighbor. Perhaps she remembered something else about the man she'd seen Debbie with. I drove to her apartment building, knocked on the door.

"Mr. Katz, nice to see you again. Are you and Debbie back together yet?"

"I'm afraid Debbie is missing."

"Missing?"

"Yes. And I believe that the man you saw her with is the one who took her."

Her eyes opened wide. "Oh, that's terrible."

"Do you remember anything else about him?"

She shook her head back and forth. It reminded me when I shook the Magic Eight Ball, desperately hoping to get a *yes* for "Will Pamela Anderson go out with me tonight?"

"Not really. He wasn't friendly as I think I told you. His clothes didn't fit properly and there was the thing on his neck."

I felt the adrenaline pour through me. "Thing on his neck?"

"Yeah. Didn't I tell you about that? Some kind of birthmark or something. Looked kind of like a...a...bee, I guess."

Chapter Seventy-One

Mickey? It was Mickey? Why would he take Debbie? It didn't make sense. Then I remembered something. The day he was drunk, he said he wanted to get Debbie back. Wanted to take her away, make her love him again. He had seemed so desperate! Did he really do it?

"Thanks a lot, Ida. You've been very helpful."

"I hope you find her."

I nodded.

I left and drove to Mickey's apartment, probably breaking every speed limit known to man and maybe a few only the aliens knew about. No one answered the door. Damn. I dashed downstairs to talk to the landlord, a fat guy wearing a t-shirt with *fat guy* written on it. *Overkill,* I thought.

He smoked a large cigar. "Do you know where Mickey in 4B is?"

He puffed on his cigar, then growled. "You a cop?"

"No."

"Moved out."

"Any forwarding address?"

"Didn't say."

I thought he might be hiding something. "Look, it's important. I think he kidnapped my ex-girlfriend and I..." What was I doing? It was useless to tell him the story. He didn't know anything. I headed toward the door.

"Marietta."

I turned back to him. "What?"

"That's where Mickey went."

"You said he didn't say."

"He didn't. But he had a map in his hand with Marietta circled.

I thanked cigar-man, asked him how to get Marietta. He picked up a pencil and drew a map on a napkin that had held something greasy. I dashed out to the car and began driving.

Why was Mickey going there? I didn't know. I did know I had to talk to him, find out what was going on. All a dying man can do is grasp at straws. Actually, I never really understood that expression. You'd think a dying man would have more important matters on his mind than what to use to drink his beverage.

It occurred to me that maybe I didn't know Mickey as well as I thought. He had seemed different that day we had spoken, more intense, like there was another side to him—an evil side. Was Debbie in danger?

It took about an hour, but finally I reached the lovely town of Marietta. It was small with numerous shops lining the streets—a bakery, a video game parlour, a hardware store, to name a few. There were only a couple of people out and there wasn't a car on the road. However, for some strange reason they deemed it necessary to have a crossing guard. He sat at the curb reading a magazine and drinking a can of Yoo-Hoo.

The Watkins Hotel stood on the corner. With it's neon lights, it looked like it had been built in the sixties. I pulled open the heavy wooden door and it creaked. When I entered I could see that at one time it might have been a first-class hotel, but now was in disarray—peeling wall paper and a faded carpet that had probably felt the footsteps of a million bad shoes.

I walked over to reception and talked to the woman there. The name plate on the counter said that she was *Harriet* and I've never known a name plate to lie. They're good that way. Wrinkles filled every nook and cranny of her face and maybe some of the crannies had two. She was probably around eighty, yet had this vigor about her.

"Welcome to The Watkins." What a voice—soft and mellow like a love song. Guess that's why she was in reception. "How can I help you today?"

"Do you have a Mickey Harrison staying here?"

"Mickey? Mmm, don't think so. At least I didn't check him in. Let me see if he's here." She began riffling through pages of the large book sitting on her desk.

"No, sorry, I don't see anything. You might want to talk to Jay. He's night shift, comes about six. Sometimes he forgets to write names in the book. He's getting to be that age."

What was Jay? A hundred and two?

"Maybe you'd like a room in the meantime." She stared at my face, distraught. "You look like you might need freshening up."

That made me feel great. An eighty-year-old woman thought that I needed freshening up after a forty-five minute drive.

I had to stay. I had to find Debbie. I just hoped I wasn't too late.

Chapter Seventy-Two

I had no clue where Mickey and Debbie might be, so I had to hang around until Jay came in. I spent the day in the town square. A sculpture of Thomas Jenny, the founding father of Marietta sat next to a fountain. I guess just in case he got thirsty. Beside it was a well-kept garden with sunflowers and pink roses. Several shops were in walking distance so I headed over to the Quarter Store.

There were loads of knick-knacks in baskets and all with signs reiterating that they were only a quarter. I looked for that one item that would change my life. I found one, but in the end decided that maybe I could survive without a soap dish that attached to my belt. I mean, I'm all for cleanliness, but I didn't think that would go with my bad boy image. I left and the cashier threw me a grimace. I could understand that. A guy comes in the quarter store, looks around for twenty minutes and doesn't buy anything. How cheap can you get? Maybe I should have gotten the soap-dish belt.

Later that night, I headed back to the hotel to see Jay. A thin man, he kind of resembled a pencil that had grown a moustache. I may have been right about him being a hundred and two. He sat in an old rocking chair, reading a crinkled copy of *People* magazine from 1971. I'm sure he had a wealth of knowledge about the Doobie Brothers.

"Can I help you?" he said, a dour look on his face. He popped something into his mouth, started chewing.

"I'm a private detective." I took out my PI card and held it in front of Jay. He looked at the photo on the card, then at me. He seemed to like the photo better.

"I spoke to Harriet today and she said I should ask if you rented a room to a Mickey Harrison."

His hands seemed to move independent of each other like one was a Republican, the other a Democrat. "Oh, the orthodontist. Yeah, yeah. He didn't get a room here; he wanted to go to the Williams' Mansion."

"Was he with someone? A woman?"

"Didn't see one. Could have been in the car, I guess."

"How did this guy seem?"

"What do you mean?"

"You know, calm, worried..."

He moved his head an inch to the right, mulling something over. Finally he spoke. "Guilty. You know like he'd done something wrong or—"

"Where is this mansion located?"

His voice suddenly took on a conspiratorial tone. "I think, maybe I've told you too much already. You know, I'm kinda like a doctor—have that confidentiality thing."

I brought out a fifty and saw his eyes light up like a nuclear power plant. "The Williams' Mansion is owned by Stan Williams, the richest man in Marietta. He rents it out for special occasions."

He told me where it was located, and twenty minutes later I'd arrived. It was a large black circular building in the middle of no-where. This man liked privacy. There were no windows and no other houses around it. Its only neighbors were ferns and squirrels.

I walked around the mansion and didn't see any cars. When I knocked on the door, no one answered. I pulled out my carver and slid it into the lock. A moment later, the door opened.

There were large chandeliers hanging down from the ceiling, and a spiral staircase off to one side. I could see its appeal for Mickey. In some ways, it resembled Mickey's old house, only a higher level of class. But then it dawned on me that he was out of work right now, and didn't have money to pay off his gambling debts. So how could he afford to rent this place? Mickey had secrets I needed to unravel.

I walked upstairs and checked out several rooms. All empty. No furniture, nothing on the walls, no evidence of anyone living here.

I was about to head back downstairs when I heard the door bang open. I crept over to the edge of the staircase, looked down. It was Mickey and behind him Debbie, all tied up. Although I saw it with my own eyes, I still couldn't believe it. Mickey was a lot of things. I just couldn't believe he'd added kidnapper to that list.

And maybe something far worse.

Chapter Seventy-Three

I thought those bad thoughts about Mickey until a third figure followed him into the mansion.

"Don't try that again," the man said to Mickey as he locked the door. "I'm gonna make sure the ropes are tighter this time."

Mickey grimaced. "I was hungry. You kidnapped me before lunch. Aren't there rules in the kidnapping business? Like grab people after lunch so they don't get cramps."

"Fine, I'll get you food," the man said with a flourish of his hands. The kind of flourish that only an actor makes.

Joe. Joe had been behind it all. He pushed Debbie onto the couch, then began tying up Mickey. When he finished, he moved him onto the couch as well.

Joe seemed different than before. Not so much in the way he looked, more in his posture. Rim-rod straight. He seemed more natural, more real, as if Joe had actually been a part he'd been playing.

Mickey stared at him. "Hey, I just noticed you have that bee thing on your neck too. Maybe we're related."

Joe laughed. "Related to you? Not a chance. I had a tattoo artist engrave that thing on me yesterday."

Mickey did a double take. "Why?"

"So people would think you had taken the girl."

"What?"

"Never mind."

At times like this I wished I believed in using guns. And if that were the case, I also wished I had one.

I had been wrong about Mickey's involvement. It was Joe who had kidnapped Debbie and Mickey. But why?

Joe went to the kitchen and took a plate of sandwiches from the fridge. He walked back into the living room and placed the plate on the table.

A moment went by, then Mickey started jabbering. "We can't eat if you don't untie us. Joe grunted, then untied their hands, but neither one even looked at the food.

Debbie started gesturing, her hands moving fast, fingers wide open. "You're nuts, crazy." Joe's face turned angry red and he brought out a gun. "If I were you, I'd calm down, lady."

Mickey nodded toward Debbie. "Yeah, Deb, you might want to take it down a notch. We don't want to get our host angry."

Her arms flopped down to her sides, defeated. "Nothing will happen, he needs us."

Mickey looked over at Joe for confirmation. "Yeah, you do need us, don't you?"

Joe shrugged.

Mickey's leg started to shake.

"I really didn't need the girl. I could have let her go. But now she knows too much. It's you I need, Mickey."

Mickey stared at him, his leg still shaking. "Why would you—"

Debbie gasped, then her hands started flying around again. "Haven't you been listening, Mickey? He's the Orthodontist Killer. You're an orthodontist. He's gonna kill you."

Joe, the Orthodontist Killer? I was in shock for a moment, then it hit me. The wax that the police had found didn't belong to an orthodontist, but to an actor. Actors use wax as part of their make-up when they appear in plays. Joe had obviously accidently left it at that last crime scene.

The imaginary light bulb above Mickey's head suddenly came on. "You know, Joe, I really haven't worked for a while. So, technically I'm not in the orthodontist field anymore. It wouldn't do much for your rep to off me."

Joe laughed. "Don't worry, you'll always be an orthodontist to me. Even when you're dead—-which will be soon."

Mickey gulped loud enough I could hear it all the way upstairs.

"And by the way," continued Debbie, "why the heck did you kidnap me? I have nothing to do with orthodontists. I own a flower shop."

"You were bait."

Mickey's forehead creased, then a moment later, creased again. "Bait?"

Joe faced Mickey as if he were Alien and Mickey was Predator. "I thought you'd be suspicious if I asked you to drive me way up here. So I forced Debbie to write you and say she'd been kidnapped. And, of course, tell you that if you didn't come alone, I'd kill her." He giggled. He really should work on that laugh. Somehow it didn't seem right for an evil mastermind to giggle.

Mickey shook his head. "I don't understand this, Joe. I lived with you. I thought we were friends."

"Friends? With a jerk like you? Forget it. I moved in because I knew you were an orthodontist. I thought that would give me leads on all the other orthodontists so I could kill them."

I stood upstairs watching this, shocked, not just at the strange turn of events, but at the fact that Mickey came all this way to help Debbie. Underneath it all, he really did care for her.

I tried to figure out what my next move should be. Joe had a gun and if I attempted anything stupid, he could kill Debbie, Mickey and/or me. So for the moment, I decided to stay put, waiting for an opening of some kind. A few moments later, it came. A knock at the door.

Joe stood up. "Okay, meal break's over. It's a shame you didn't even eat anything." He tightened the ropes around their arms and walked them over to the area beside the stairs. He lifted a trap door in the floor, then took them both downstairs. The trap door slammed shut.

Five minutes later, Joe emerged, alone, and answered the front door. He talked to some mousy-looking guy who didn't have much of an upper lip, then he went outside. Now was my chance.

Chapter Seventy-Four

I crept down the stairs, hoping that Joe was telling this guy about his acting credentials—which would keep him bored for hours.

When I reached the bottom rung, I quickly opened the trap door and stepped downstairs. It was dark and I could barely see in front of myself. From what little light there was, I could tell the hallway was a mass of old Styrofoam coffee cups, food wrappers and cardboard containers.

My foot accidentally made contact with an empty bottle and it rolled down the hall, hit some rocks, and made a loud clinking sound. I prayed Joe was still outside the house.

I now stood in front of a door. The cautious part of my brain wondered if Debbie and Mickey were behind it and if they were the only ones. The door was open slightly and I worried this might be too easy. It could be a trap.

I moved toward the door, about to enter when I suddenly saw movement, a flash of color in the open space. I kicked the door open with my foot and suddenly, a big boulder flew out. I jumped back. The boulder slapped onto the ground, an avalanche of pieces.

When I recovered from that, I saw Mickey standing in front of me with a few rocks in his hand. A euphoric look filled his face as he dropped the rocks and hugged me.

"Thank goodness it's you, Arn. I thought it was gonna be Joe. Sorry about the rock thing."

Debbie rushed over and hugged me too.

After they un-attached themselves, I walked into the small, barren room. It too had lots of garbage on the floor. Fortunately, there was a light bulb hanging from the ceiling so I could see that they both looked okay. "How did you guys get free of the ropes?"

Mickey smirked. "He may be a great Orthodontist Killer, but he's not so good with knots."

Debbie nodded. "We used some of the sharp rocks here to cut the ropes. Then we opened the door, hoping Joe would come down again and we'd jump him."

Mickey grimaced. "Debbie would jump him. I'm having back trouble. I wouldn't be doing any of the jumping."

Debbie patted me on the shoulder. "How did you know we were—?"

Mickey spread his hands. "The man's a master detective, that's how. And a great dentist. Did I ever tell you that, Arn? All this time I sort of thought you were second rate. But you know some of my patients have seen you and they just couldn't say enough good things." Mickey was a 9.5 on the giddy scale.

Debbie grinned. "I don't know how you figured it all out but—"

Mickey grabbed my arm. "The big lug is here, that's all that counts. I guess you have the police upstairs huh."

I shook my head. "Sorry, no. They wouldn't come."

Debbie leaned forward. "So who do you have?"

I parted my lips in a sad pathetic smile. "Me."

Debbie stared at me like I was crazy. "But you do have a plan, right?"

Mickey spread his hands again. "Of course he does. He's a master detective."

I hated to break it to them. "No, not really."

Mickey's body quivered. "Give me your gun, Arn. I've got pretty good aim."

I told him about my aversion to guns. Mickey, now starting to get agitated, pounded the wall. "So how the hell are we going to get out of here?"

I approached him like he was a small child. A small child who had been raised by wolves with ADHD. "Mickey, I think we should just walk upstairs."

"Just walk upstairs. That's your master plan? That madman is up there waiting for us—"

Debbie piped up. "With a gun!"

I explained that right now he was outside talking to someone and suggested that maybe the first thing we should do is gather up some rocks. Sharp ones.

They agreed reluctantly and both picked up a pile of rocks. When they had done that, I said, "Okay, let's go upstairs and see if we can make a break for it."

Mickey's eyes opened wide. "Make a break for it?"

"What else can we do?"

I began marching down the dark hall, the others following. When we got to the top of the stairs, I pushed the trap door open and looked out. No Joe. I helped the two of them up into the living room.

We were about to make a rush for the back door when I heard a welcoming voice.

"Arnie Katz, so nice of you to join our little party."

Sometimes welcomes aren't all they're cracked up to be.

Chapter Seventy-Five

Joe stood by the open door, holding a gun. He spit, then spoke. "Okay, why don't you all sit down?"

Mickey, Debbie and I took a seat on the couch.

"This is an interesting turn of events," Joe said. "Originally, I had planned to kill one of you. But now it appears I have to kill all of you. Well, it's good practice."

No-one spoke for a moment, then I said, "So you're the one who's been killing all the orthodontists."

He bowed theatrically like an actor who had just received an Oscar. "Correct."

"Why?"

"Simple. I hate the bastards. When I was a kid I had really crooked teeth. I was in a theatre program at the Richmond School for the Arts, all set to play Romeo in Romeo and Juliet. Then the stupid orthodontist gave me braces. It made me lisp all my lines and all the kids at school made fun of me. It ruined my life." Joe brought out a tissue and wiped his eyes.

"That was a long time ago, Joe." I said. "Besides, lots of people get braces when they're young."

"Yeah, but did they look like this?" He reached into his back pocket with his non-gun-holding hand and pulled out his wallet. He removed a picture of a young Orthodontist Killer wearing enormous gold braces that actually extended out of his mouth. I'd never seen anyone with braces like that before.

"You should have sued him for malpractice."

"I told my mom, but she was too busy with her damn P.T.A. meetings and macramé classes to do anything."

He threw the picture on the ground and stomped on it. Then he picked up the picture, ripped it in half and threw it into the air. "And the damn orthodontists always have that arrogant attitude about them, 'I'm better than you. I'm an orthodontist.' I spent my whole life working out a way to get back at them all. And now I have it."

I looked at him, feeling sad for the man, even though he had plans to kill us all. "Joe, I wasn't a fan of the orthodontists either. But they have a hard job and they do help a lot of people. You can't blame them all for what happened to you."

He ignored me and put the gun down on a table. Then he reached into his pocket and pulled out a long piece of arch wire. He walked toward Mickey. "Okay, Mickey, smile. I'm sure that's the way you want to be remembered right?"

"Not necessarily. I'd actually liked to be remembered alive."

Joe began bending the wire in a half circle, then held it in front of Mickey's neck. Mickey tried to push him away, but Joe was strong.

"Listen, Joe," Mickey said, "Isn't there another way we can—"

"Can you stop talking? I'm in the middle of something here."

I used this moment of confusion to reach into my pocket. I pulled out my forceps and threw them at Joe. They hit him on the head, blood dripping out. A look of pain appeared on his face and he grabbed his head with his hands. I ran toward him, but he re-aimed the gun at me. Before he could pull the trigger, I managed to bend his wrist back so the gun pointed upwards.

I tried to pull it out of his hand, but he kicked me. I kicked back. It startled him and he dropped the gun onto the floor. It went off and shot a piece of plaster from the ceiling. He forced me onto the ground, then rabbit punched me in the gut. It hurt like hell, but I somehow found the energy to keep fighting. I twisted him onto his side and at that moment, through the corner of my eye, I could see Mickey and Debbie watching like two bored people at a cricket match. I screamed, "Could use some help here."

Each of them grabbed one of Joe's legs. It looked like they planned on making a wish. I hoped the wish was that this day had never started. But apparently it had and Joe had morning energy. He pushed Debbie and Mickey to the ground, then punched me in the face. I could taste blood. I tried to grab him again, but I felt weak, dizzy. He sprang up and dashed out the front door. What kind of vitamins was he on?

I waggled my way up and sped after him. I gave chase into a nearby forest, but then lost him. There were so many trees, he could have been anywhere. I had to stop running. I was out of breath, exhausted.

I walked back to the house, trying to get my breathing under control. I felt terrible losing him. But what could I do?

I found Debbie and Mickey sitting on the ground, both catching their breath. I was the one fighting and they were incapacitated. "He got away," I said.

"Great," said Mickey." Now, we all have to go into hiding for the rest of our lives."

Debbie tilted her head. "At least we're alive."

I nodded, happy for that, but knowing the nightmare for us and the city would never truly be over.

A moment later, the door opened and Joe stood there, with a rifle aimed in our direction.

"That was a nice exercise program, guys. But I'm afraid now we have to end the fun." He shot the gun. Mickey went down.

Chapter Seventy-Six

Joe aimed the gun again, this time at Debbie. I raced over and stood in front of her.

Debbie whispered to me. "What are you doing, Arnie?"

"The only thing I can do."

Joe started laughing. "Isn't that sweet? He's trying to save you. It won't work, Katz. After you go down, Debbie gets it."

Suddenly, I heard the sounds of a car outside.

Joe looked back. I took that moment to run toward him. I flew onto his body and we both fell to the ground. He still had morning energy, but I had something stronger—revenge energy. I started punching him in the gut. I could see by his face, he was worn out, too tired to punch back. I hit him on the head and he blacked out.

I stared at him, not believing that it was finally over.

I could see the relief in Debbie's face. "Is he…"

"No, I don't think he's dead. Just out."

"What about Mickey?"

I looked over at Mickey's lifeless body, then turned to her. "I'm sorry, Debbie."

She started crying. I put my arms around her. We stood that way for a few moments consoling one another.

Then I heard a voice.

"Hey, guys."

Debbie and I were both too afraid to look. When we finally did, we saw Mickey standing and smiling.

Debbie rushed over and hugged him "Mickey, you're okay."

"Yeah, he missed me by a mile. But I pretended to be dead to save everybody. Great plan, eh?"

I nodded. "Yeah, uh, wonderful plan, Mickey."

We talked for a few moments, then the door sprang open and a big sweaty man walked in. Another man followed. He took a rope out of his pocket and began tying up Joe.

"Hey, Arnie," the sweaty man said. "Guess, we got here a little too late."

"Hi, Mr. Rodrico, Robert. What are you guys doing here?"

"I told you, Arn, you're family and we keep track of family. I found out from one of our mutual contacts, Benny Gordon, what you were up to and I thought you might need a little assistance. I had Robert follow you, then call me when the time was right."

"Thanks, Robert."

He came over, put his arm around my shoulder. "Welcome to the family, PI." He tried to smile but some of his lip got stuck in his teeth. He'd have to work on that.

Rodrico held up his hand. "We'll dispose of the body for you, Arn. That's our speciality." He winked.

"He's not dead, Mr. Rodrico."

"Not yet, he's not."

"Actually, it might better if you gave him to the cops."

"Sure, whatever you say, Arnie. But first, we'll get him to understand that when he tangles with you, he's tangling with a family member."

Robert began dragging Joe outside to the car. Joe had come to and started screaming. "Katz, don't let them take me. Who knows what they'll do?"

I shrugged. "Sorry, it's out of my hands."

Robert left, and Mickey walked closer to me. "Aren't you going to introduce us, Arn?"

"Oh yeah, sure. Mr. Rodrico, this is Mickey. And this is my, uh, friend, Debbie."

Rodrico kissed her hand. "Charmed, my dear." I could see Debbie was charmed back.

"Thanks for helping us, Mr. Rodrico."

"No problem. Anyway, I gotta go, Arnie. I had one of my associates inform the police what was happening up here and they may come at any moment. I wanted to have backup just in case. I probably shouldn't be here when they arrive, though. You know the police and me, we don't get along so good."

"I nodded."

He left and drove off.

Chapter Seventy-Seven

The next day, there was a major press conference at City Hall. Walter Dennison, the Mayor, pinned a medal on my chest. Apparently, Rodrico, through one of his associates, had let the police know that I was a hero, that I had single-handedly taken down the Orthodontist Killer. I didn't see myself as a hero, I was just trying to save my gir—ah—a friend. But the attention was nice. Of course, there were lots of questions from the press. And, as always, the heads of the police department weren't too happy with a dentist solving a major crime that they couldn't.

I headed to my office to get back to some good old dentistry. As usual, it was a packed house. But I couldn't blame Tanya this time. She said with my new found notoriety everyone wanted to meet the dentist who had captured the Orthodontist Killer. Luckily, Dr. Michaels was there to help.

And who was first up? You guessed it—The Slatsky Kid. He looked up at me with his wide eyes and wind tunnel hair and said, "How did you captu—"

At that moment, Tanya came running in. "You've got a phone call, Arn."

I smiled at her. "Nathan and I are talking, Tanya."

"I think you should take this one."

"Alright. Hold that thought, Nathan." I picked up the phone. "Hello?"

"Hey Arnie."

"Dad?"

"Yeah, son. It's me."

"What is it? You know I haven't changed my mind about being a law—"

"I just wanted to tell you...I couldn't believe what I saw in the paper this morning."

"Dad, look—"

"Son, I want you to know how proud I am of you. I guess I didn't realize how good you are at what you do. I shouldn't have tried to turn you into something you're not; that was wrong. You have to do what's inside your heart. I love you no matter what you do."

I was touched. "I love you too, dad."

"Why don't we go out for supper, Friday."

"No lawyer friends or shenanigans?"

There was a pause. "Just you and me. I want to hear all about your detective business."

"Sure. See you Friday."

I hung up, happy that he and I had reconnected. Although I had a hunch this honeymoon period would be over soon and he'd start a new campaign of trying to get me back into law. Probably on Friday!

I finished up with Nathan who asked three hundred questions about how I caught the Orthodontist Killer. I didn't mind answering them this time since he seemed to have a new respect for me.

Actually, there'd been lots of changes this week. Leo popped the question to Tanya. She loved being asked, but I haven't heard what she's going to do with that yet.

Mickey, now free of all his gambling debts, was able to get a loan and start his orthodontist clinic up again. And Debbie went back to running her flower shop. She and Mickey aren't talking at the moment.

As for Debbie and me, I really don't know what's in the future. But she wants to talk to me about something today.

THE END

ABOUT THE AUTHOR

 Steve Shrott's mystery short stories have been published in numerous print magazines and e-zines. His work has appeared in ten anthologies—two from Sisters-in-Crime (*The Whole She-Bang*, and *Fishnets)*. He was a winner in The Joe Konrath Short Story Contest (2006). His comedy material has been used by well-known performers of stage and screen (including Joan Rivers and Phyllis Diller) and he has written a book on how to create humor. As well, he teaches humor writing at various real world and cyber schools (such as Savvy Authors and The Romance Writers of America). Some of the jokes he wrote for Phyllis Diller are featured in an article about her in the March 2007 issue of the *Smithsonian Magazine*.

Steve's first book for Cozy Cat Press was *Audition for Death*.

www.ingramcontent.com/pod-product-compliance
Lightning Source LLC
Chambersburg PA
CBHW050402260626
47156CB00003B/842